Zoran Torma

STORIES

Published by:

FriesenPress

Suite 300 – 852 Fort Street
Victoria, BC, Canada V8W 1H8

www.friesenpress.com

Distributed to the trade by The Ingram Book Company

To my son and my wife

CONTENTS

GIVERS AND TAKERS

My mother Rachel married a man sixteen years ago and divorced him only one month later. A year after that she gave a birth to me. No one knew who was my father, and Rachel wouldn't tell.

I was ten when we moved back in with Sam, Rachel's father. Bubbee passed away suddenly, as everyone was saying, and Sam bade us to live with him. The house, this big red brick abode with huge, old evergreen trees, with a coach house and a high brick wall for a fence, was my grandfather's home and now it is mine. I tend to occupy the two small rooms in the attic where I sleep and draw and from where I can see far across the roofs. I go downstairs to eat and watch the movies. Sometimes I make a simple kind of cookies with sour apples or plum jam (Rachel's recipe, the only one she knew), chicken soup (the way Sam made it) and flat bread, (my own invention), or some other simple dish. Then I go to the basement, a warm and dry place, to watch eight-millimeter movies that Sam shot over so many years and so long ago. I watch the movies while nibbling, smoking and occasionally sipping Sam's plum brandy.

In spite of all these years, the movies have kept their colors. They show my Bubbee and the endless blue of the sea and the sky. My Bubbee is always in a pretty summer dress. She walks down a steep trail, she sits at the Pantheon's base, she rides a donkey, she stands by the French Opera House. And all the time she smiles at the camera.

My Bubbee was a ballet dancer. That was how they met, my Bubbee and Sam: in the theater in Belgrade. She had a difficult repertoire, Sam said so many times. Her body is graceful, but strong. Her face is oval, beautiful and small. Sam and Rachel don't appear in the films even once.

Sam was a concert pianist back in Belgrade. He had a very short career. He was in his early twenties when he gave two concerts in Moscow, two in Budapest and one in Lille, France. Then he married Bubbee and they moved to Canada before Rachel was born. Rachel said they had to hide from the Russians. She said Sam was a spy and I believed her.

I tried to get that from him. By the time I was twelve, I grew tall and strong and I played on the school baseball team. Sam liked it. He came to watch me play almost every game, and Rachel came perhaps twice. After the game Sam took me to the deli and we stayed there for hours. Once I asked him about the spying business:

"I am not confirming or denying it, Maxi. That means something, doesn't it?"

But that wasn't enough for me. I wanted him to tell me: Yes, I was a spy, or: no, I wasn't. So I kept working on it.

Sam had a talent for genuineness. When Bubbee died, he not so quietly whistled a Bach tune with a very fast tempo through the whole shiv'ah. At last one of the visitors dared to ask:

"Did Danah like Bach?"

And Sam said:

" He was all right, of course. No, she liked me to whistle. She needed to know that I was always somewhere close by."

Sam held himself a religious man. He was a regular in the shul, but then he would unexpectedly go bowling three Friday nights in a row. He convinced me to have a Bar Mitzvah. Rachel lived that year in Florida with her new boyfriend.

"Now, that Rachel's eloped, you and I will have more time for ourselves. First thing, we'll get you ready for your Bar Mitzvah."

He taught me a bit how to read from the Torah. I learned as much as I could and it didn't go smoothly. But the party was a success.

"Maxi, I am so proud of you, so proud," he said to me and hugged me.

Then he sat at the upright and played a couple tunes. No one knew about his pianist past and they were all in awe.

A week later, as we were sitting at the Shabbat table at home, he said to me:

" I wasn't really a spy. I did a thing for the Brits, back in the day. I carried envelopes a couple of times back and forth. You know, playing piano I traveled a lot. It was supposed to make me less suspicious. Also, I spoke languages."

"I sort of knew you were a spy," I said. "How many languages do you speak?"

"Five."

"But, if you were caught, you would have to go to jail?"

"I'd probably get the death penalty then. Then again, I knew a very good lawyer. A couple of them. Still, it was a crazy time. Plenty of innocent people were killed. I was at least guilty."

"Did you want to be a spy, or someone made you?"

"I wasn't a spy. They asked me and I agreed to do them a favor. You know, they paid well. I needed the money, I wanted to get married."

"How much?"

"Quite a bit."

"How much?"

"You are a pisser. Cannot remember the exact amount. It was enough for us to get married."

When Rachel came back from Florida, she was very unhappy because she wasn't told upfront about my Bar Mitzvah, she said, and she decided not to talk to Sam. Sam gave her some money the next day. She went out shopping immediately. When she came back in her new and beautiful summer dress, all in flowers and vine, and in dark red sandals, she was cheerful. She also brought three boxes filled with pastry and custard pies. That night, we sat on the floor around the coffee table, and, with the radio playing quietly, Rachel told us about her Florida days. She was tanned, looking strong and healthy and she was funny mocking her ex-boyfriend.

That summer we spent on the beach, in the movie theatre, or in the back yard, making crapes on an old hot plate and talking. Sam was telling his European stories, how he called them. They were funny and full of twists. We talked about moving back to Belgrade, to Dubrovnik, spending the rest of our times on hot send of the Adriatic Sea. I knew it was only talks; still, it was exciting to imagine all those places, that kind of life. And then, toward the summer's end, Rachel became suddenly ill. We were going to the movies and we had to turn back, toward the hospital.

Sam and I waited until the nurse came out and told us that Rachel had to stay. We walked slowly home.

"I always meant to show you something," Sam said.

We turned onto a steep street and we kept climbing to the top. There, we found a long and narrow lane with wild chestnuts on both sides. The crowns were reaching over and touching, making a canopy. We walked under it. Here and there the moon would shine through.

"Danah and I used to come here. We would walk for hours under these chestnuts. She loved this street, summer or winter. In winters all these branches held enough ice and snow to make you wonder and perhaps start believing, you know," he said and he pointed toward the canopy few times, but I knew he was pointing toward the heavens. "I always said I would take a photo, but I never did. Just look at this. It would be even more beautiful if it were in bloom."

At the end of the street we turned back and stood there for a while. A sudden gust of wind blew into our faces and the whole canopy shook and rustled.

"Let us go home. Early tomorrow we are going to take Rachel out of that hospital."

We returned the next day, early in the morning. A nurse was paged and she quickly came to greet us. Then she motioned with her head to follow her to a small, out of the way hall. There, she told us Rachel died last night. She died from sepsis.

We sat shiv'ah alone. The days were still warm, but it was cold in the house. We sat in the kitchen, by the wood stove. We ate in silence stale bread and tcholent that Sam made.

It was the following year, two days before Rosh Hashanah that a turtle-dove moved in under our roof. It cooed loudly and often, and almost into the winter. Then one morning it suddenly stopped. Sam passed away in his green armchair, sitting by the window, just before dusk that day. He closed his eyes and his head slipped down on his chest. I sat across him by the darkened window glass for a while and then I carried his body to bed. It felt weightless in my arms.

NINA

Her name was Nina and she was thirty. I was four and I was a picky eater. She found me on the big field framed by locust trees, close to the river, not too far from our house, just across the main road. My mother took me there before lunch, or dinner, to fly a kite. It was supposed to improve my appetite, yet it never did. I could never make the kite fly. I didn't have any interest in flying kites, I guess. So, after the debacles, I was given only the sustenance I would accept: vanilla pudding and noodles from the soup. On rare occasions, I would agree to take a slice of an apple or a wedge of a pear.

The church bell sounded noon when Nina came across the field in a flowery summer dress: red and golden flowers on a cream-colored background. And under that creamy and flowery cover, even from afar, I saw the turquoise blue of her undergarments. She had dark red sandals and her toenails were of the same color. She walked slowly toward us.

She greeted my mother first. Then she squatted in front of me and her long and dark hair, her narrow face, her voice and her breath were at once impressed into my heart. I glanced down her dress and I saw her white breasts pushed up by her knees, underlined by the blue lace. She asked me for my name and about my kite, but I stood in front of her stunned and mute. My hearing and my vision became inconsistent and blurry. She reached for the string spool by my mother's feet and she opened her legs for a very short moment. I caught a glimpse of her soft thighs, all the way down to the blue silk strip, and the black hair coming out on each side. The whole landscape turned around me and I felt faint. I quickly looked back to her face. Her lips were moving, she was still talking to me, but I couldn't grasp one word. My mother answered instead. She explained the connection between the kite and my pale complexion. Nina was standing now with her flowery underbelly close to my face. She took the kite and she called me to follow her. We walked toward the middle of the field and away from the trees, all tall and old, with big, dangerous crowns.

She made the kite fly right away. It climbed steadily on the wind and soon it was a dark speck against silver and white clouds. Suddenly, she bent over me and embraced me from behind. I felt her warmth and her sweet smell. At first, we held the spool together. Then, she carefully gave it to me. I was surprised and frightened by the strength of the pull at first. But then, against all my instincts, I surrendered my self to it: I let myself be connected with the heavens. She kneeled by me, whispering in my ear, telling me when and how to tug. Sometimes the tugs had to be slow and long, other times they were quick and decisive. After a short while I felt tired and in my belly I felt for the first time a strange kind of emptiness.

After a while, my mother decided it was time to go home and Nina invited herself. Chicken soup, stuffed zucchini and poppy seed strudel were already on the table. The small pot with milk was on the stove and the pudding powder was ready by it, just in case I would throw a fit. Nina washed my hands and she sat me at the table, then she scooched by me. Without asking, she put in my plate chicken soup. Only a few noodles made in the plate, but I didn't protest. I ate it all. After the soup she gave me some zucchini with yogurt and after it I was served a thick slice of the strudel. I ate the poppy seed filling from it and some crust.

Nina came, first to the field and then to our house, all that summer. Toward the end, when the days became colder and windier, my mother stopped taking me to fly the kite. Soon after, Nina stopped coming to our house. I waited for her and I hoped. I found a dubious consolation in drawing Nina in her summer dress. I hid my drawings and I didn't dare to ask about her.

One night, it was already cold enough to get the tile stove going, my mother told me, while she was putting me in my bed, that Nina had moved back to the Capital City. I waited until I was alone and then I whimpered a bit under the heavy duvet. The flames from the tile stove threw reds and yellows on the wall and the ceiling. Waves of warmth and the smell of burning coal came over me from time to time. A new feeling, a feeling that has never tried me before, squeezed my lungs and my heart. Nina's betrayal, I thought, broke me, it made me yearn forever.

And I never stopped longing. After all these years, in cold autumn nights, sitting by my wood stove, I still pine just the same over the summers that had forever passed.

THE TILE LAYER

Sarah, my daughter, she is a childless widow and she lives far away. Rachel, my wife, left me for Max, my colleague and friend, a sworn bachelor, twenty years ago. And then, only two years later, she left Max for a younger fellow from the British Isles. That is where she lives now, I imagine.

And Max, he passed away. Last fall I found his obituary in a month old newspaper. Although we didn't speak much after we retired, he was the only friend I had, despite Rachel.

Then, there is Tommy. When I sold the house and moved into this apartment, I hoped he would never find me. Tommy is Rachel's nephew and, when he was a little boy, I took care of his fevers. He was one sickly boy. Untamable too. Once he broke his arm after he fell down the stairs in the Museum of Modern Arts. When he was little, he called me Uncle Daniel and he was telling everyone he was going to be a doctor just like me. Later, when he grew up a little, he called me Uncle Danny and even later, just Danny.

I called him Tommy. And Tommy never became a doctor. Instead, he became a pathological liar and a thief, a very bad one at that. A couple months before I sold the house, he came, after a long absence, to visit me. He asked to stay for a couple of days and I let him. Those couple of days turned into a couple of weeks. I gave him a few dollars, so he would leave. Before he left, he took my brandy, a big wedge of Edam and the smaller of the two silver menorahs.

Max's passing disturbed me a great deal and I couldn't stop thinking about him. October started with cold rains and wind. An unusually calm and warm day toward the month's end made me decide to go to look for Max. It took me the whole morning to ready myself. I went through all four shoe boxes filled to the top with old photographs. When I was done with it, I called for a taxi.

It already darkened by the time I've got there. I was not sure why, but I pretended I came for a walk in the park across the cemetery. I asked the driver if he would come back in one hour. He said something to me, but I didn't hear him. He skillfully turned his taxi around and left. When I couldn't see his taxi light anymore, I crossed the boulevard and stepped onto the paved path in the cemetery.

I walked to the newest part where I though Max would be buried. I walked from one fresh grave to another, the soil on them appearing to be just turned over, worth checking. I did that for some time, confused, trying to remember the obituary, but to no avail. The night was closing in on all of us, the alive and the dead, and I rushed back. When I reached the gate, my torso was sweaty and cold and I regretted my decision to come to look for my friend.

The taxi was waiting at the cemetery entrance. I walked quickly toward it. I recognized the driver who just dropped me off:

"Who died?" the driver said.

"My friend. A very close friend," I said.

"Ah. So, what are you going to do? Everybody dies. Everybody. Where to?"

"You remember where you picked me up? There."

He turned the car around. We were picking up speed:

"I didn't think you would come back," I said.

"I told you I was coming back. I had to go for gas. I was almost empty."

He looked at me in his rear view mirror:

"Of course I was coming back. It is night, it is cold and you are an old man," he said.

"You are not much younger," I said. It made him laugh.

"Anyway, I didn't find him. I didn't find Max," I said.

"Max is his name?"

"Yes. I didn't find his grave."

"I will drive you there tomorrow. Days are much better to look for dead friends."

"I'll remember that."

We stopped behind a long line of cars:

"Movie's finished. Everybody goes home at the same time. So, what time tomorrow?" he said.

"I don't know. I might not go tomorrow. "

"Why not? I will pick you up earlier this time. Maybe around eleven. The radio says the weather is going to be even better than today: sunny and calm. What else you have anything to do anyway? Come, find your friend."

He was right: I didn't have anything to do. I looked at him from my back seat. He was a short and chubby man in his mid fifties. His cheeks were unshaven and he looked tired. He patiently waited for the traffic to start moving:

"And I also don't have anything to do but to drive this taxi. I'll pick you up tomorrow around eleven."

I agreed, knowing I would not follow it through.

"It is not only the movies. Something happened. An accident. People are crazy how they drive."

We sat quietly and motionless for a while. Then he said:

"Let me tell you a story. It's about my Uncle. You are a very sad man, you remind me of him."

My Uncle, my father's half brother, was a hard workingman. Beside the chimpanzee, he lived alone. He was a tile layer, a very good one. He laid tiles in government buildings, in rich people's homes. He wanted to get a good, young wife, so he worked hard, saving every copper coin he earned. He made lots of money, but in the mean time he had ruined his knees. He made himself a cripple: he could barely walk. And if you have to use two canes to drag yourself around, it's very hard to find a young woman to marry you. So, there was a widow who came back to the village from the city. My Uncle started to talk with her cousin. And who knows how it would finish if it wasn't for the monkey."

"A chimpanzee is an ape," I said.

"What?"

"A chimp is an ape, not a monkey."

"Yeah? Whatever, ape, monkey, it's the same. He hung himself."

"Who hung himself?"

"The monkey hung himself. He hung himself in the tool shack."

"The chimpanzee hung himself in the tool shack? Was it an accident? I knew of a dog, a boxer, who accidentally hung himself on a gate. His collar had too much slack."

"No accidents. Everybody knew that. There was a pile of tiles under the monkey and a rope around his neck. You see, my Uncle's Father hung himself also. Long before the monkey did. The people saw it as very bad karma. The widow didn't want to marry anymore."

"Perhaps she didn't want to marry because of your Uncle's knees."

"Perhaps, but no. It was because of the monkey. The monkey made her change her mind."

"So, what happened then?"

"Then my Uncle hung himself too. In the same tool shack."

"Really? Because of the woman?"

"No, of course not. Because of the woman! Because of his knees. I told you, he couldn't walk anymore."

The traffic started to move again. Soon, we drove by a car with its hood opened. A woman was sitting in it alone.

"This is what you get when you want to drive an import. American cars are the best," he said.

I've never gone back to the cemetery. I called the office there and they told me that Max was buried in the old part of the cemetery. An old plot he had reserved long ago. So, I let my good friend be in peace alone. I think about him often, but to this day I didn't go to visit his grave.

And I thought about the chimp. Last spring I found an envelope with Tommy's handwriting among my junk mail. He wrote to me a long, rambling letter from jail and the first chance I had, I went to visit him. I found him disheveled and in a bad mood. He knew I would come, he said. We talked a bit and I left with him some money and two bags with kosher cold cuts and chocolate cookies. I gave him my address too. A couple of months later he was released and he came straight to me.

I put down some rules, knowing he'd never quite stick to them, but it didn't matter to me for as long as he was pretending he was trying. Then I made him take the equivalency courses by paying to him a monthly salary, pending he passes the courses. It worked. Another year and Tommy will have his high school diploma under his belt.

I spend my days reading, doing usual chores. Tommy also reads, he reads his textbooks, and he helps around the apartment. We keep ourselves busy. When we really don't have anything to do, we sit idle around. Then Tommy asks me to examine his chest. He has chest pains, he says. So, I take my stethoscope out, while he takes his shirt off. His body is small and skinny and pasty. Sitting like this across me, he reminds me of the little Tommy I examined so many times, so long ago. After I volunteer my doctor's opinion confirming his good health, Tommy asks me to tell him stories about his childhood, about his mother and his aunt. I remember everything, but I tell him only the good stuff. In the end, already deep into the night, he asks me to tell him the story about the chimpanzee and the tile layer. I do it gladly. And I expand it every time, pretending to look for a plausible explanation of the ape's despair. He laughs and I laugh with him, although we both know it is an unfortunate, tragic story.

ROSE

A strange sentiment about the world, veiled with pathos and a persistent need to be always somewhere else, I inherited from my mother. And because I have it, I prefer to spend my time alone, or, once I let myself be involved, I find myself unavoidably on the opposite side of everything.

I also inherited from my mother the place among Gypsies that I've lost over time. They lived by the kilns and down, toward the dugouts. Some of the men, those young and strong, worked there molding and baking brick. The others sang and played accordions and violins from one village to another, from a town to a town. The women, the young and the old, they read cards and palms for a cigarette or two, or for a couple of coins.

Rose was tall and skinny and beautiful in her layered, colored skirts and with her gray hair, thick, rich, freely falling over her straight back. She was old and she would come to our home from time to time, always with one or two of her great-grand children, who were always girls, always close to my age. My mother would set the table for all of us to eat first. After the meal, Rose and my mother would drink coffee, smoke and throw cards. I was supposed to play with the girls, but I would let the girls play with my toys without me.

I was overwhelmed by the Rose's presence. I felt like she put a spell on me and I needed to be near her. I listened attentively her argentine, deep voice. The words seemed to have a different meaning, mysterious and soothing at the same time, when she was saying them.

I was almost six when I opportunistically asked Rose, as my mother stepped out, to read from my palm. She took my hand without hesitation and looked carefully over my life and love lines. She studied my future, I thought trembling. Finally, she said just before my mother came in:

"If you live through your seventh year, you will live passed your fifty-seventh."

I pulled my palm out of Rose's, and I ran to my room. I threw myself on my bed, excited with such an outlook and that it came from the woman I unconditionally adored. Fifty-seven seemed like plenty and a long time away, I thought. I didn't think for a moment about my seventh year. Only once when it was a long time gone, I was already fourteen, I remembered it. And then all I could have recalled, vaguely, was a bike riding mishap. Could it have become the misfortune costing me my life?

My mother and Rose are a long time gone. I moved to a far away city soon after my mother passed away and our house was sold. I kept in touch with our friends for a short while after I moved away, but the affections and the curiosity we had once for each other withered away gradually, but quickly and forever. And to befriend someone, I found it to be in bad taste, inappropriate, hard and unnecessary. I've chosen to be friendless.

I am fifty-five today. My editor wished me a happy birthday this morning. And she was the only one to do so. I was touched with her sincere voice over the telephone and I wanted to tell her about Rose. Perhaps I thought I needed someone to share with me my suspense. Coming closer to my fifty-seventh, I ask myself all the more now what will happen once my guaranteed life expires.

MAYTAL

It has been scooped
My red hollow
And the insides tremble
In the cold and sorrow and now
There is almost nowhere to go.

By the eye's edge
Lie the numbered days
In the high grass of the coming summers
We will lie under
Dry and hurt.

How quick this turn was!
The first cry echoing still
Always present yet it came
Time to do nothing.

I wrote the poem because of Marjeta, yes, Maytal's other name was Marjeta, and for Maytal. I wrote it for Maytal out of the narrowness of my soul and she converted the poem into the tongue of her childhood that same night. And later, during my spells of despair, derangements and self preserving lies, she would recite it to me slowly and with a whisper, always in the lowest register of her argentine voice:

Je to smeteno
Mé Rudé Prázdno
A nitro se třese
Zimou a v děse a ted
Skoro není kam jít
Hranou oka
Dny sečteny
Ve vysoké trávé blízícího léta
Pod nimi budeme položeni
Vyprahlí a bolestní
Jak rychlý ten obrat byl!
Ten pravní výkřik ješté daznívajíc
Stále přítomen a přec
Ten čas nic nedélání se dostavil[1]

I recount these stories to Deborah and to her son Avi during the long Shabbat nights. I remember everything, but some of it I tell only with a sigh and silence. They listen and understand my every pause.

Maytal came to Canada on a commissioned rusty steam ship. She arrived in Halifax from Hamburg, from the Zoological Gardens DP Assembly Center. Her Zapadocesky Kraj family, the Aunt and her son, left her in Hörsching Camp almost a year earlier. They settled in Hörsching after three nights and four days of walking on side roads, of crossing pastures and hops fields.

Streams of gunfire and thunder of cannons could be heard for days. They were coming from afar, accompanied with the breathless stories of men and women passing through the village, talking about the already liberated south. The German troops, those who were left behind, gradually began to abandon their posts altogether. Retreating, they took with them men who were not careful, or smart enough to hide. The moment the Aunt heard the first burst of gunfire, she hid her son in the house. She hid all his belongings as well, and she made a narrow cot under her mattress, just in case. She told Maytal to smear herself with the soot and to put the burlap robe on again.

Toward March's end the gunfire, although sounding closer, died out. The news spread the war was over, yet no one truly believed it. Then, it was already April, two artillery shells hit the village. They came early that Good Friday morning, with a whistle and from nowhere. One fell on the

---

1   Maytal's translation was lost. Much later, I asked M. H., a Czech fellow, to translate the poem for me. He agreed under one condition: to be acknowledged for it with his initials only.

piglet roaster's house, the other straight into the pond by the sty, throwing the water and mud mixed with duck feathers and carcasses over the sty wall and the grass, deepening and widening the hole quite a bit. The Aunt didn't bother to see what just happened. She, mute, made dough, quickly flattened it into three flat breads and put them in the oven. The boy packed his rucksack with all colored and adorned eggs and a strip of bacon, then he ran to the sty and let the sow and the chicken out. By the time they were done packing, the flat breads were ready. The Aunt threw water over the fire in the stove. The three of them took the shortest way out of the village, avoiding the already abandoned German posts. They headed south.

The first day there would be a dark silhouette, rushing, same as they were, across fields, close to the woods when possible. The following day there were more people steadily pushing toward the border, walking in a double file on the road, moving aside only to let a truck or a jeep pass by. The Aunt decided that the three of them stay off the road. She allowed only for rests long enough to take a bite or two and a sip of water. The main meal was before sunset. They ate eggs, bits of bacon and the flat bread. After the meal, they drank a strong tea, falling into a shallow sleep, cocooned by each other under a tent wing, before night took wholly over. The third day, not noticing, they found themselves a part of the mass.

Apart from a sound of a jeep, or a truck driving by, or an occasional plane flying low, sometimes above their heads, sometimes in the distance, it was quiet. As they neared a small village by the border, a truck stopped in front of them. The driver motioned to the Aunt to approach, offering a ride. He already had a few passengers sitting by him in the cabin and few at the back. The Aunt recognized a woman from their village, a distant cousin. She was sitting by the driver, holding her little boy in her lap. Tired and hungry, they climbed up on the back of the truck, not saying anything to the familiar passenger.

The truck took them straight to the camp, passing the broken files of people. It drove through the wide open gate and stopped in the middle of the big yard surrounded by barracks. Over there, by the wooden wall, sat a group of strange looking men. Maytal stared at their sunken cheeks, toothless mouth and bulging eyes. Some men didn't have their shirts on, showing their rib cages and arm bones, soaking the sun in, smoking cigarettes, talking. When she heard them speak Yiddish, she hastily started to inspect their faces. She madly looked for her father.

"They are sick, the poor men," the Aunt said.

The first night in the camp the three of them slept together under the open skies, on the clean, dry hay, covered plentifully with horse blankets.

"We will go back home soon," the Aunt said. "And you'll go back to your mother and father. We'll all go home."

Maytal had her eyes closed. She thought of the men by the barracks: "They are not there anymore," she said.

" Who knew something like it was going to happen again?" Deborah said. Yes, who knew?

Early next day Maytal put her name and the names of her mother and father on the Red Cross list. There, in a small, cold and badly lit room without a window, a woman at a new and shiny desk, too big for the room it was in, asked Maytal in fluent Czech if she was a Jew. Maytal leaned on the polished veneer, leaving her fingerprints on it. Her throat narrowed. And all she could do was to nod her head. Then the woman asked her if she would be ready to go to America or to Canada, if an opportunity for it presented itself, and Maytal nodded her head again, choosing Canada, remembering the vast icy landscapes in Jakub's books and the label on the thermos her father bought for the picnic.

The days in the camp started to turn into a long wait for everyone. Ever since she moved to the old barracks, Maytal surrendered herself to exhausting walks and the dreamless sleeps that followed. Or she would join the women at the laundry trough, or in the kitchen, washing and cooking for days, or she would climb up one of the watchtowers and gaze at the people below. The Aunt and her son stayed in the barracks closest to the Red Cross quarters. There, in those barracks, stayed people who hid from this peril as one would hide from a summer shower. They spent their time telling each other frightening stories about mad Russian soldiers, about Captain Czerny, about a new war that just began between the allies. The conscription of young men was on its way again, they were saying and it was hard to tell what was true and what was not.

When Maytal began to disappear, the boy sulked craving her presence. As the autumn approached, the boy sunk into silence, he stumped around aimlessly and heavily. So, one morning, very early, only days before Rosh Hashanah, the Aunt and the boy woke up Maytal to bid her farewell. The Aunt sat on the edge of the bed. She still called Maytal Marjeta. She spoke in half voice, at times overtaken by the revving of the truck engines. Maytal couldn't understand every word, so she sat up, showing her readiness to listen. But the Aunt didn't have much more to say. She and the boy had to go back to their home, and that was all.

It dawned on Maytal that she had been waiting for this since they'd arrived to the camp a wave of abashment came over her. She searched for the right words to respond, to say that she understood everything, but she couldn't find any.

Somebody outside, a duet, started to sing the Rosh Hashanah song under the small, high window. The weak, soft voices, mixed with occasional engine grumble, persevered with their, to Maytal familiar, timbre:

Shana hal'cha Shana ba'ah
Ani kappai arima
Shana tova lecha abba
Shana tova lach ima
Shana tova, Shana tova.[2]

Avi chanted the lyrics with me.

Maytal hadn't heard the song for a long time. She smiled.

"I didn't know the occupation would last this long. If I did, I'd never take you from your mom and dad. You must know this," she kissed Maytal and put the necklace with the stone into Maytal's hand. The boy clumsily kissed Maytal's forehead, then he walked away between the bunk beds, toward the doorway, expecting his mother to follow. And she did.

Maytal wanted to call after them, but the soft ropes of lethargy wouldn't let her move. She sat on the edge of her bed for a few long moments and then slowly walked to the door.

The Aunt and the boy climbed up into the back of the truck and disappeared behind the heavy canvas flap. Maytal stood on the wooden threshold, waiting for them to appear one more time. The trucks were now out of the gate, revving, picking up speed. After a short and straight stretch of the road, and before the line of old poplar and bush, which shielded the road from a clear view, there was a mild curve followed by a decline. The trucks drove through the curve and down the hill, their sounds muffled, dying out.

Maytal stayed in the doorway for another minute, then she went back to her bed. The pendant was still on her pillow. She put her head by it. Now, when the diesel fumes were gone, she could sniff a faint, pleasant smell. It came from the soap in the just unloaded boxes. She closed her eyes and she saw a dale. Tall grass churned left and right, up and down. With the gusts of wind came voices. The whole view lit itself with a strong light and Maytal opened the bottom drawer on the commode in the house in Prague, to look for her sunglasses she never had. She peaked under large and heavy linen, under the towels, under her little summer dresses she thought she forgot. Her mother sat by her on the planked floor:

"You don't have them. You never did, my Maytal," she said.

"I never had them," Maytal heard herself saying. "The sun shines strongly, and it shines in my eyes, my mother."

"Look away, my Maytal. Close your eyes. Cover your face with your palms."

---

2   One year has passed / A new year is coming / I will raise my hands / And bid a Happy New Year / To mother and father.

She and her mother were laying on the hot sand in *Žluté lázně*[3]. Her father stood above them. The water drops on his arms and on his fast breathing chest focused and reflected sunrays. He just finished his swim across the river and he looked very content.

Only few days after the Aunt and her son left, Maytal was called for her photos to be taken. A cousin, certain Mrs. Beth I. from Canada, was Maytal's guarantor. It was early autumn when the news arrived, but it took a long wait, all the way to the winter, before Maytal left the camp.

The time came and Maytal was given the traveling instructions and the documents with a photo of her in it, a small cardboard coffer painted dark brown, filled with food rations, some extra clothing, a soap bar and a tooth paste without a tooth brush. The documents for Mrs. Beth I., sealed in an envelope, were in the inside pocket of the lid. Maytal was told to wake up early that morning, long before the sunrise, but then she had to wait, together with boys close to her age, until late that afternoon.

The boys carried the same coffers Maytal did. The three of them walked out through the gate led by an old, short man. He was dressed in a heavy Wehrmacht overcoat and a pair of new soldier's boots. Maytal and the boys stumbled in silence over the frozen land, as if they were rushed and quieted by someone and something else but by themselves and the cold cutting air. The train was a thick black line in the distance, steaming and whistle calling, as if threatening to leave without them, so they rushed and stumbled even more, breaking into sweat. They quickly left the old man far behind.

Maytal climbed up into the first car. It was crowded and stifling inside. The young bodies, all young men, the lives that stubbornly resisted the false gods and demons of the insane, broken humanity, and who came out on the other side as victors, were now emanating that victory with the warmth of their blood and breath, with their loud voices and harsh odors. They offered, wordlessly and indifferently, a place to Maytal. And she accepted it in the same way. She pushed her brown coffer under the wooden bench and then she took off her heavy winter coat. She wedged herself between the wall by the window and a boy, a sickly child, who was asleep sitting.

The landscape changed as the pale sun fell behind the dark line of the far forest. Then everything disappeared in the winter darkness. The train stood still, steaming, promising to move. Suddenly, the small and faint lights of torches started to flicker and dance, far in the darkness, and Maytal thought that more people were coming to board the train. As they came closer, they turned toward the locomotive and could not be seen anymore. Then a pair

---

3   The Yellow Spa, the beach in Prague, on Vltava

of lights appeared on the other side, closing in fast. It was a military van. It stopped not too far from Maytal's window and she could see it.

Someone outside shouted back and forth in English. Then a boy came in, stumbling from the adjacent car, making his way through toward the next. He spoke Yiddish and he said to Maytal, since only she paid attention to him, that a woman had passed away in his arms, and that he was the one who alarmed the crew. He motioned toward the window and there, in the van's headlights, Maytal saw the two uniformed men carry a stretcher with a small body on it, covered with a gray blanket. They passed through the headlights quickly, disappearing behind the opened doors at the back. Then there was a sudden long whistle, the train shook and the night in the window started to move, leaving everything behind. The young men became livelier, as if they just woke up. They started to talk more loudly, mixing Yiddish with Czech. At once, everyone was eating boiled, unpeeled potatoes. A young man offered a potato to Maytal. She took it without saying anything.

The boys, the young men, they were skin and bone, but they still looked tough and unruly and it puzzled Maytal. The child leaned more toward her and his head fell on her arm. She thought to wake him up and feed him the potato, but instead she leaned back against the seat and the wall and she cradled him. Soon, the only sounds were those of the iron wheels hitting the rails' joints and, occasionally, of the whistle. By the time the train made out of the long curve, turning north, and before it crossed the bridge, everyone was in a hard sleep. Everyone but Maytal.

Maytal recounted her stories slowly and not in any exact order. Her sentences were often scarce and short and the weight of their meaning relied upon her eyes and her breath, upon the closeness of her body, it relied on the smell of her thick hair, dyed golden blond, and the curve of her rouged, full lips. Now, without Maytal beside me, my words are only the mumblings of an alchemist, the spells recited over the concoction this life is, perhaps in hope that the accounts will be set straight. Deborah and Avi listen quietly, unavoidably late into night. As the candles run out of wick, Deborah sends Avi and me to bed. Then she lies on the couch in the living room. I hear her reciting blessings and prayers.

I met Avi first. I met him last year at the shul, just after the Sukkot. A tall and handsome young man, in his late twenties, childlike, I sat by him during the *maariv*. He smelled of clean clothes and margarine. He davened whispering the prayers and the blessings too slowly, so he had to rush, cutting them short all the time. But he was the first to standup for the *Amidah*. There was no room behind or before us and we took our steps in one place. We whispered: *Adonai, sfatai tiftah ufi yagid tehilateha...* He bent at the knees and he bowed vigorously, smiling at me. I smiled back. Then, the next day, the

Rabbi, a young, stout and strong man who just arrived from Philadelphia, asked me if I needed help with the house chores and he recommended Avi's mother Deborah. They lived in the shul basement, "A temporary solution," the Rabbi said, and I offered them to share Maytal's house with me.

Maytal called my apartment a studio. She loved to be among my paintings, she repeated so many times. All around us on the walls and on the two easels, and leaning against the scarce furniture, hanged and stood the large canvases, most of them triptychs, with dark forests under heavy firmaments, with deep black, lifeless and perilous bodies of water, with mountains made of iron and snow, both spoiled with rust. They reminded her of the landscapes on her Moon, she said, pointing at the hidden pendant on her chest. The other paintings, the paintings of Maytal, I conjured them in her absence and she had never seen them. I hid them from her, I hid them from everyone. The world in them is bathing in lights and hues of ultramarines and Prussian blues, cadmiums and vermilions, pearl whites and gold. Framed with vines pregnant with unknown, inviting fruit, Maytal stands on the top of a hill, while behind her, far down in the valley, behind many layers of atmosphere, and following the narrowing road, stand big linden crowns in full bloom. A serpent like river is to Maytal's left, or to her right, mirroring the clear skies. Her hair is to her shoulders and it has its natural, hazel hue, the one it had when I saw Maytal for the first time. She wears lilac and white silk I had painted selfishly over her bare body afterwards. Her ears are adorned with pearls or with gold and rubies. She always looks straight into my eyes, their irises and pupils mirroring my venerating face, while her lips are just beginning to smile. In her hands she holds the Moon.

Maytal helped her mother wash the ten glass jars and ten bottles, the family heirlooms used for the preserves and now the glass was sitting, all upside down and tightly packed, in a shallow saucer pot on top of the stove. After the Shabbat, her mother and father would cook and strain tomato and finish the peach and plum compotes. And just before the candles were to be lit, two men, the father's friends from afar, knocked on the door and, as soon as they stepped in, they joined the blessing.

After the dinner, the four of them stayed seated at the table. Maytal sat between the stove and the couch and listened. They spoke Yiddish, but Maytal could barely understand what the two men said; their Yiddish was different. She listened to her mother's and father's questions, she looked at their pale and disbelieving faces, she saw her mother and father getting angry and scared. The candles burned down, and the mother lit another two.

Maytal fell asleep between the stove and the couch. Led by the harmony and rhythm of the voices in the kitchen, she dreamed herself at the promenade. Someone was saying it was the time to hide. Hide your hands and legs?! Did he say 'hands' or 'heads'? Hide, hide, hide! Did he say 'legs' or 'pegs'? Maytal turned around to ask, only to see that she was alone at the desolate, unknown place. Something started to run toward her. She could hear its breath and claw against the cobblestone and her mother's scream. She begged Maytal to run. Run, run, run, but Maytal could not make herself move. At once the scream became too loud, too real, and it was followed by a sharp, crashing thunder. Maytal opened her eyes in terror. The two men, her mother and father were standing above her. All around them was broken glass.

No one could tell what made all those jars and bottles fall like that. Perhaps the earth under the house settled, perhaps the last drop of water, the only morsel that kept them together, dried. The father picked Maytal carefully up. Then he quietly carried her to bed. When she woke up in the morning, the two men were already gone. Maytal didn't ask about them. She didn't ask about the glass either. After that night a pressing veneer of obscurity settled in their house. Her mother cried often, and her father, trying to hide it, cried too.

Maytal was three when her Zayde passed away. The last day of *shiv'ah*, she found her father sitting on Zayde's bed, a tall and narrow divan in the smaller of the two small rooms in their house. On the bed were two goose feather pillows, tall and big, and an old duvet neatly folded and put at the foot end. Maytal climbed up and sat by her father.

Tears wetted his sunken, unshaven cheeks. She had never seen her father cry before and she wasn't sure what to do. She sat close to him and she put her hand on his. Her father didn't respond. She looked around the room, ready to wait for him to stop crying. She looked over the books on a small shelf, counting them: *eins, tsvey, dray, fir...* Under the small table with a drawer lay Zayde's slippers, neatly put away. On the table was a bag made of black silk plush, adorned with an inscription embroidered with golden thread. In it were, together with Zayde's tefillin and tallit, the two photographs, taken only weeks before the Zayde passed on. The whole family, the four of them, was on those photographs. Maytal asked to see them. She pulled on the father's sleeve, she shook his arm, but he was not answering.

Maytal left the room troubled. Her mother was stretching dough on the kitchen table and she offered to Maytal a slice of sour apple, already peeled and cut, darkening on the plate, but Maytal frowned at them. She went out in their small backyard and sat on the granite threshold, hot from the sun. The linden tree in Jakub's yard cast its shadow and fragrance over the wooden fence. She sighed. She wanted Jakub to be in his back yard, so she came to the fence and put her face against the narrow slit between the planks. She called: "Jakub, Jakub," but her voice was not more than a whisper. She saw

Jakub's wooden horse and his small chair. At the other end of the big yard were white linen sheets drying on the clothesline at a standstill, deceptively tight, as if they were pretending to be screens in the movie-house. She called again: "Jakub, Jakub," and her voice came out even more quietly. Then she heard her father in the kitchen asking about her. She rushed back to meet him, but instead of going in, she sat again on the threshold. Her father came out and sat by her. He had in his hand the two photographs from the tallit bag and the one, hand colored, which Maytal had never seen before:

"This is me. I am three years old here. Same as you are now," he said.

Maytal looked at the small, serious face of the boy with yarmulke and tzitzit under his short coat. He stood alone, serious, in front of a golden gate, a backdrop in a photographer's studio depicting the entrance to the First or Second Temple. Maytal looked up at her father's face, then she looked back at the boy's. She searched for a likeness, but she couldn't find any. It became apparent to her that her father had lost, perhaps right after the photograph was taken, something very important. And she felt helpless and scared for him. She climbed up into his lap and he cradled her readily, tightly and gently at the same time.

As Maytal and I walked down the alley, a girl, who could have not been more than twelve, and an older woman, walked toward us. The girl was blind. She had big sunglasses and a long, white stick. She held the woman under the arm. That evening, back in my apartment, Maytal told me:

It was a late summer afternoon, only days after the visit of her parents' friends, the night the glass broke. She and her mother were returning home when they saw a young woman with a little boy walking into a clutter of scaffolding and heaps of sand and gravel in the front of "The English Court", the hotel being rebuilt and renewed that year. They both wore black armbands. The woman wore sunglasses and with one hand she held her boy's hand, and in the other she had her white stick. The woman was blind. She had to be the little boy's mother, Maytal thought.

The woman patiently tried to feel the way with her stick, but wherever she probed, there was an obstacle. They went from one heap of sand to another, from a scaffolding post to the wall. The boy was stumbling over the rubbish, holding his mother's hand, following trustingly. They finally stopped between a heap of fine sand and a pile of wide and long planks, not knowing where to step next. The boy stood by his mother patiently. At last, a man hurriedly came out from the hotel door hidden by the scaffolds, possibly one of the hotel personnel. He quickly lifted the boy in his arms, and at the same time he put the woman's hand onto his shoulder, and he led them out of the predicament.

As they walked, Maytal leaned against her mother's strong thigh. They cast one elongated shadow over the cobblestone. The shadow danced, darkened and faded over the uneven surfaces of pavement and brick walls. It fell between the cracks and into small holes, came nearer on the wooden fences and disappeared in the opened gates. Maytal looked up at her mother. Nothing is alike to itself from one moment to the next, Maytal thought. The world keeps disappearing, forever and irrecoverably, from an instant to the next, only to make space for the one that randomly follows. But at the same time, surrounded by this randomness, she sensed a stagnant chasm of the never changing constant, an infinite, omnipresent entity, as if it was here to underline and remind of the absence of any purpose. Maytal's whole body, her mind and heart, slowly pressed inward, collapsing on itself under this thought. The feeling of utter helplessness, the same one she had while sitting with her father on the threshold, only this time it was stronger and more defined, came over her and she started to whimper, while her mother held her hand, hot and sweaty, tightly yet gently, as if she didn't want Maytal to ever let go.

It took time to arrange Maytal's hideout. A family friend, a Jewish man whose wife was a Czech, found a woman, the Aunt, who was willing to take Maytal. She lived alone with her son in Zapadocesky Kraj, on a small farm: a large garden and a few acres under barley, all adjacent to their humble house and a sty with chicken, ducks and a sow.

The night of Maytal's departure everything happened hurriedly and few words were exchanged. Her father and mother walked Maytal out on the street in the summer night lit only with the moon. They didn't have any baggage on them. It was already sent away, taken to Maytal's new home beforehand, all her necessary belongings, except for the evidence that Maytal was a Hebrew. So, there, on the summer night street overwhelmed with linden scent and lit by the moon, Maytal left her name behind too. The Aunt, as the woman wanted Maytal to call her, waited for them a few houses down the street. When they approached, she called Maytal Marjeta. The mother hugged the Aunt, just as she did the first time they met on the edge of the woods. The four of them stood there close to each other for a minute and then the father and mother turned back home. Marjeta quietly started to walk with the Aunt toward the train station.

Her father said, as the Shabbat was coming to its end, that they would go on a picnic early in the morning. When Maytal woke up, she found her mother and her father sitting on the threshold, reading newspapers, waiting for her. Her mother already packed food in a large wicker basket. A friend's car was parked on the street. After the breakfast, unusually quick and silent, they packed the baskets and blankets into the car and set themselves on the road. They drove to Zbiroh and then out of Zbiroh to the edge of the woods, where they finally stopped. The trip took couple hours of slow driving.

It was Maytal's first picnic. A dusty road, the road that brought them to the site, cut through the clover and barley fields. After the clover's greens and purples and the gold of barley, far in the distance one could see the line of the village houses and the church bell-tower. The three of them found a spot at the edge of the woods. Maytal insisted to carry the heavy basket from the car all by herself. The mother spread a tablecloth over the thick grass and then she arranged the food on it. They started to eat right away, as if they didn't have breakfast at all.

They had the Shabbat dinner leftovers. A bee would land on the challah, on pieces of carp, kishka slices, but her father and mother let it walk freely over it, so Maytal did the same. Whiffs of the greenery and sunrays filled Maytal's lungs and head, as the food filled her stomach, and she felt sleepy. Her mother spread a blanket for her, but Maytal wanted to lie on the grass.

She faced the sky and a new view opened in front of her. The vastness of the bright blue spilled all around and at once she felt as if she was going to fall in it. She closed her eyes quickly, grabbing for the grass, her heart beating loudly. But it wasn't the high layers of the atmosphere that truly scared her. It was the face behind it, the true one, dark, cold and infinite, whose presence she felt very clearly. She kept her eyes closed.

Her mother and father talked quietly, a bee buzzed here and there, a tree crown rustled, a turtledove called. Maytal could see the long house of the Kayak Club and the people on the beach and she knew it was *Žluté lázně*. She looked around herself and she saw that she was floating on the river. She never swam before, but she let herself courageously turn back onto her tummy and she started to swim. She cut through the warm and cold, elusive water, just like her father would, strongly and decisively, with her face in and out. She moved fast, leaping, often not knowing the difference between the water and air. Her breath was calm, her arms and legs tireless and she felt as if she could swim like that forever. Then she heard fast, swooshing sounds behind her. She wanted to turn and see who was in her wake, but she couldn't find anything sturdy to push herself off. Her mother called her name and she woke up. A tall, slender woman was walking toward them, smiling, wishing them good morning, commenting on the fresh, almost cold gust of wind that just started to gather.

It was the Aunt. She wore a white blouse and a long, dark blue skirt. Her golden hair was held back in a simple braid tied in a small kerchief. She carried an elongated, pear shaped wicker basket over her arm. It was topped with mushrooms. Her father stood up quickly and shook hands with the Aunt. Her mother jumped too. She hugged the Aunt as if they were old friends, then the three of them sat down. The Aunt sat on the grass by Maytal. The church bell rang the noon hour from afar.

Maytal liked the Aunt at first sight. She liked her courage to gather mushrooms in the forest all by herself. A wooden, broad handle of a big knife stood up in the basket among the mushrooms. It was yet another reason for Maytal to admire the Aunt.

Her mother served coffee from the big Thermos Bottle, Co. Ltd. of Montreal, Canada. They sat on the blanket and they started to talk softly, kindly to each other. They asked the Aunt about her son, about the village and Maytal quickly lost interest in their conversation.

In the meantime the shadow from the woods crept over them and Maytal felt cold. She walked out of the shadow, out into the part of the field bathed in sunrays. Then she walked further away, first down and then up the small hill. From there, far on the road, she could see an ox was pulling an empty cart. A small, dark figure of a man walked by it. Nearby and in front of her, two young sparrows were leaping from one red clover flower to another. Maytal ran toward them. They skillfully escaped. Then a turtledove cooed from afar, from behind the village, behind the picture of green, gold and blue bursting with sunlight, churned by the sudden gusts of wind. She turned around. Her eyes needed to adjust to the darkness of the shadow. Her mother and the Aunt were sitting across each other, with their profiles markedly different. Her father was sitting with his back to Maytal, he also a silhouette, skin and bone, in his puffy white shirt, with a cigarette between his lips, unlit and superfluous. A feeling of uneasiness came over Maytal. She ran back into the shadow and sat by her father. He put his arm around her and kissed the crown of her head.

It was time to eat again. The Aunt made fire in no time. She fixed a small pile of dry grass and twigs and she lit it with a single match. Then she broke a few branches over her knee and carefully put them on the small flames. She said to Maytal to sit on the other side, because of the smoke that would start rising soon, and then she put two mushrooms on a plate. She put in Maytal hands the big knife from the basket, telling her to cut the mushrooms.

Maytal never had a knife in her hands before, not even the small one her mother used only to scrape the salting board. Now, before she had time to think about it, she held in her hands the big, sharp, heavy blade. She carefully put the cutting edge against the mushroom and the steel cut through it with uncomfortable ease. She cut through the other mushrooms and she carefully gave the knife back. The Aunt put the halves on a tiny spit she made from hazel twigs. Then she showed Maytal how to hold it over the fire. Maytal turned the spit slowly, watching the mushroom meat sweat and sizzle, watching the elusive flames dancing above the ember. The smoke curved away from her just as the Aunt said it would, and Maytal knew she was a beholder of the looming change she sensed the night she was sitting between the stove and the couch, the night she woke up by her mother's scream in the heap of broken glass.

They walked fast. The Aunt held Maytal's hand, smiling at Maytal from above. They turned into the street by the Jewish cemetery. A man on a bike pedaled tiredly toward them. When he passed by, the bell on his bike gave away a quick, unintentional ring and Maytal turned her head toward the sound. There, in the cemetery gateway, stood her father. She freed her hand and ran back. She ran fast by the brick wall. But, as she was nearing, she saw that no one was there. The gate she pushed to open so many times before looked unfamiliar now. It was ajar. She was scared to open it more. The Aunt came behind her slowly. She smiled and she took Maytal's hand. Her palm was still hot and sweaty. They started to walk again toward the train station, while Maytal cried silently.

Maytal never took a train before. As they walked by the locomotive, the steamy breathing and puffing was interrupted by the sharp sound of the whistle. This startled Maytal and she stopped crying. They quickly climbed up into an empty car. The Aunt sat by the window, wanting Maytal to sit by her, but Maytal sat across.

The Aunt talked softly. She was promising that the trip wouldn't take long and that everything would be all right. Maytal spoke only when she had to. Under the dimmed coupe lights the Aunt resembled Myrna Loy, Jakub's favorite. She took out from her small purse a slice of poppy seed strudel, wrapped in butcher's paper, and she offered it to Maytal. Maytal refused it and the Aunt immediately put the strudel back in the purse. Soon, the train started to move. Before they left the station, Maytal felt sleepy. She leaned against the wall by the window and she closed her eyes. Just as the train picked up speed and the wheels fell into the right rhythm, just as she started to fall into a deeper, dreamless sleep, there came a long curve in the tracks and the metal started to shake and squeal. It woke her up and she peeked. Myrna Loy had her eyes closed too. What would Jakub do if he were sitting across Myrna Loy like this? First of all, he would take the strudel. He liked poppy seeds. "*Barukh ata Adonai Eloheinu melekh ha'olam hamotzi lehem v* poppy seed strudel *min ha'aretz,*" whispered Maytal, almost without a sound. That was what Jakub would say before biting into it. He would never miss a blessing. Maytal smiled. The train pulled out from the curve and it was regaining its rhythm and its speed. She fell into sleep again. This time she dreamed of her father and Jakub. The two of them stood at the beginning of the cemetery alley. It was daylight and the gate was wide open. They called her to come in, but when she made a step toward the gate, the gate closed shut. She looked between the cracks and she saw her father and Jakub walking down the alley. She wanted to call to them, but her throat narrowed, she couldn't make any voice. They disappeared between the tombstones and the evergreen trees.

Maytal woke up in the Aunt's arms right after they came off the train, but she pretended she was still asleep. The train station was a small, unlit house. A short, paved road turned quickly into a wide and long, unpaved one. Soon, they were passing by small houses, haystacks and gardens under the full moon. Dogs barked somewhere in the distance, proving their presence. Beside the Aunt's steps, it was the only sound that broke the silence.

They soon arrived to the house. The Aunt put Maytal on a narrow bed in the kitchen and took her, and Maytal's, sandals and socks off. She covered Maytal with a clean bed sheet she brought from the bedroom and a lavender scent filled the air. Then the Aunt removed her own clothes. She did it quickly, in one motion, all at once. Her body was strong, made of sinew and heavy bones. Her chest was flat and in between her two large areolas there was the third one, bigger and darker. Maytal, hidden by the shadow, opened her eyes wide. She held her breath. The Aunt stood like that, her body and hair darkened by the moonlight. She untied her hair and it fell on her back. Then she leaned forward, grabbing water from the pail by the door. The middle areola separated from her chest, and before her hair fell over it, Maytal saw that it was a pendant hanging on a thin line. The Aunt drank thirstily. The moonlight fell on her thick, golden hair, on her narrow face and strong, long neck and she didn't look like Myrna Loy anymore.

"Lilith," Maytal whispered and smiled. She was another of Jakub's favorites.

The lavender soothed Maytal's tired heart, the straw mattress made her feel as if she was lying somewhere in a clearing. She closed her eyes. The white and the blue of an endless sky spilled over her, while someone called her name. She stood up and looked around. By her feet was a heap of shiny, colorful pebbles she didn't want, yet she took them. They felt hot and heavy. She opened her palms to count the stones: "*Eins, tsvey, dray, fir ... eyn, tsvey, dray, fir ...*" Her hands were getting hotter and heavier and she needed someone to tell her what to do. As she turned her eyes toward the window in the house in Prague, she saw her mother's face close to hers. She and her mother were sitting at the table, counting the pebbles: "*Eyn, tsvey, dray, fir ...*" Her father sat by her and kissed her cheek, removing the pebbles from the table with a quick swipe, which were now snail shells, letting them fall and bounce on the kitchen floor. This startled her and she lay down in her bed, covering her eyes with her palms. Her father and mother lay down by her, with their faces very close to hers. They whispered to her in Czech and in Yiddish, but she couldn't understand what it was they were saying, although she knew they were words of comfort.

The Aunt was German on her mother's, and Czech on her father's side. She spoke both languages to her son. The two horses they used to keep trampled the Aunt's husband. This happened on St. Wenceslas Day, three years before Maytal's arrival. An artillery shell, fired by the Czechoslovakian Army, landed too close to the stall and startled the horses. The hole the shell made was still there, wide and deep, always filled with rain. The Army had been on maneuvers ever since, the boy said. And it seemed that all that was left of his father was one photograph. The photograph was too small to be hanged yet it was faithfully there, above the bed in the mother's bedroom, under yellowed glass, in its thick, wooden frame. The man stood there in the full uniform of an Austro-Hungarian soldier, with the butt of his rifle against his right boot.

The farm was a one-hour walk from the picnic spot. Maytal's mother and father drove there in the friend's car every weekend. The car would arrive always late in the day, yet before the Shabbat was over, and Maytal would hop in it right away, straight into her mother's lap. Then they would slowly drive toward the dirt road and then toward the town. There, they would take a room in the only hotel. All three would lie down on the bed, with Maytal in the middle, and talk. Maytal talked the most. She talked about the Aunt and the boy, the room that was given to her only and about school after it had started. She always asked about Jakub, until her mother said that Jakub moved away.

Sundays, just before sunset, they drove back to the wood's edge. The Aunt would be waiting there, as if she had never left, with basket filled with wild fruit, flowers, roots, and mushrooms. And, as the car drove away, Maytal and the Aunt would start their walk home, carrying the basket between the two of them.

The boy gave himself the duty of preparing Maytal for her place in the new school. He warned her about the cruelty of some teachers and pupils, offering her his protection, if not from the teachers, then from those unruly oafs and snotty mutts at least. Maytal liked that he gave them such names. He was not scared of anybody, she thought. His strong face, with piercing blue eyes that would turn gray when angry, his broad shoulders and tall stature were contrasted by his soft voice. Maytal was attracted to that softness and the way in which he pronounced some words, making them sound new, unknown, as if she had never heard them before. But because of his practical nature, he would always run out of stories too quickly. Then Maytal would ask him to read from the textbooks and he would readily read for hours. She listened with undue attention, and not to learn, she sensed that she knew much more than he did, but to prove to him, and to herself even more, with this innocent affection her readiness to befriend him forever. As she befriended Jakub. And Sam. And me.

More Germans came to the village that autumn, a month before Rosh Hashanah. They kept a small regiment at first, mostly in the barracks they built by the drying kilns. Now they increased their numbers. They had control over the post office and the train station and they put ramps and guards on all four roads to the village. Maytal was puzzled by the ramps. She couldn't understand why anyone would need to guard the roads. The number of soldiers tripled over the years, but their presence didn't show to be a burden.

Because the Aunt felt safe, she kept taking Maytal to the edge of the woods. They walked there every Saturday afternoon, as usual. They often crossed paths with the soldiers patrolling in a group of four. The Aunt would be always the first to salute. Sometimes she would even stop them for a short talk. They responded readily, talking back loudly, with unexpected, yet natural politeness. One time a soldier, a young man, gave to Maytal a piece of milk chocolate. He smiled at her and he put his hand on her head, talking to her in German, asking about her age. Maytal understood it through her Yiddish, but she said only one bashful thank you. In Czech.

The Aunt and Maytal picked hawthorn berries, red gooseberries, mushrooms, crabapples, wild pears, fingerhuts, red and yellow, hardhay, flowers and roots of herbs which names Maytal couldn't remember. They waited. They would stop themselves in the middle of a step or bow, thinking they heard the familiar whisper of the car engine, listening for it. By the end of October Maytal said she didn't want to go to the woods anymore. It cooled down and the drizzle turned into a wet, heavy snow. Winter had arrived.

The boy and Maytal brought into the house a small fir tree they cut together. They propped it in the kitchen, between the window and the bed's foot end, jamming the stump into the hole of the thick wooden cross the boy pulled out from under the bed. The Aunt took a box from the commode in her room. In it were twelve large glass balls, wrapped in thin, soft, white paper. The Aunt carefully unwrapped one by one each ball and hanged it on the tree. The red, blue and green glass, with silver and white glittery twirls on it, was delicate, as if it could brake on its own any time. And this fragile look added an immaterial, hard to measure value to it. The adorned fir changed the kitchen into a place of expectation and magic and Maytal liked it at once. The boy looked at the decoration in awe too. His father bought it in Prague, he explained to Maytal.

The day before Christmas the boy and Maytal went for their piglet roast. There was an old man, not too far from their house, a neighbor, who ran a small bakery and who roasted holiday piglets for a small fee. Maytal and the

boy walked through deep snow, cutting across the field toward the neighbor's house, which at first appeared to be closer than it was. Maytal arrived
there sweaty and tired.

The roasted piglet, still on the spit, was waiting for them thrown on the
makeshift table, wrapped in a white linen sheet impregnated with grease.
The neighbor and another old man were quietly sitting between the square,
big oven, made of brick and mud and the hole filled with amber. They
smoked tobacco rolled in newspapers, sipping a clear liquid from small pear
shaped bottles. Two piglets, most likely the last two for that Christmas, were
still on their spits over the ember. The little carcasses sweated and dripped
into the fire: whoosh, whoosh. The boy took off his mitten and he paid the
neighbor with two copper coins. He picked up the thick end, letting Maytal
grab the scorched and pointy wood and they started to walk back.

The sun still shone strongly and now it shone into their eyes. The dead
weight soon began to overwhelm her, just as did the smell of the burned
grease and meat. She stumbled over the icy crust, turning her face away from
the wrapped carcass, from its heavy odor. The boy's strong legs grabbed
forward. He led steadily, carrying the bandaged meat with an undue hurry,
pulling Maytal who was now barely hanging on the spit. She was sweating,
breathing through her mouth, but determined not to give up.

When they arrived, Maytal had cold shivers. She sat by the stove, pale
and absent. The Christmas tree was now also decorated with a myriad of
small candy canes. Maytal looked at their red twirl and she tasted the sweetness all over her mouth. She craved one, but she didn't dare to take it off
the tree.

The smell of the grease on her hands was making her even sicker and she
stumbled out to wash it off with snow. She rubbed her hands crouched by
the threshold and they quickly became dark red, almost blue. Yet, the layer
of grease and the smell of it were still there. The boy came out with ash in his
hand. He gave some of it to Maytal and than he started to rub his hands too.
The ash helped. When Maytal slowly stood up, burning, to walk back into
the house, the boy took out a candy cane from his pocket and gave it to her.

Maytal waited in Hamburg for three months to board the ship, and now
it was a warm, pleasant summer night when she found herself at the railway
station in Hamilton. An older woman with a wide brimmed lady's hat, and
dressed in a bright and modern summer gown, waited for her:

"Call me Savta Beth, or just Beth," she said.

Maytal looked at this fine, kind woman, she examined her face, her
whole elegant figure. Her body was standing and moving in the way, Maytal
thought, she unintentionally had forgotten over the years in Zapadocesky
Kraj. Maytal's mother stood and mannered like this, Jakub's mother too.

And all the women Maytal used to see on the promenade outside of Josefov, where she and Jakub were taken for ice cream and long strolls after the movie show, they presented themselves in this way: gracefully and kindly. Maytal decided that the place she came to was a good place. She smiled.

Savta Beth said:

"You know I am not your cousin? I lied. I had to. I just had to bring you here, to bring somebody here," she said and gently hugged Maytal, taking her carefully toward the exit. They rode a taxi car from the railway station to a big house on Beulah Avenue.

"She was a good woman," Deborah said.

Yes, Savta Beth was a very good woman.

Savta Beth's husband volunteered in WWI, but, according to the British Army, he died of gun wounds somewhere in Palestine, soon after the Jordan Valley battle, or, almost two decades later, he was killed in the battle of Brunete. Savta Beth received two letters informing her about her husband's demise: one from the 20th Battalion of the London Regiment, two years after WWI was over, and the other from the British Battalion, quite a bit later. Each envelope contained, beside the consoling words, a photo. On each photo a man in uniform struck a pose, but in neither of them Savta Beth recognized her husband.

She never remarried, and not because she suspected and perhaps hoped her husband was alive. She had discovered a new kind of life without a man in the house. She grew all by herself the small textile store her father started, and she inherited, into a respectable garment outfit. Just before Canada joined WWII, she sold the store, together with the building, and she bought a house in Hamilton's quietest neighborhood. The house was tall and wide, with big front and back yards, hidden and protected by old maples. From the main entrance, a big double door with beveled thick glass in round lead frames resembling vine and flowers, Maytal saw the specious hallway tiled with brown, red and white pattern tiles. It led to the kitchen and sitting and reading rooms.

Maytal and Jakub were only two years old when they were introduced to each other and became inseparable. That winter Maytal spent in Jakub's spacious house. They sat at the big table in the reading room for hours, leafing through the books with print's reproductions, through the atlases of the night skies and old and the new worlds. This was where Maytal heard for the first time about the wind rose, the oceans and sailboats, the Cosmos and the infinity. Jakub encouraged her to peruse the shelves. He talked about his favorite books and people in a instructive way, possibly imitating his father. There was never only one open book in front of him. He wanted to be a serious boy, letting his mischievous, funny face out only when he thought it was unavoidable or necessary. His mother was expecting to deliver any day, so she came to check on the two of them only before mealtime, letting Anezka, the maid, do most of the supervision. As soon as his mother left the room, Jakub would take a chair pillow and put it under his sweater. Then he walked around the table with his hands on his hips, with an expression of pain on his face, aping his mother's voice:

"Jakubchek, Maytalchek, you must eat now, children. Jakubchek! Maytalchek! Eat! Eat! Eat!"

When his mother was in the hospital, delivering, he said to Maytal that he knew how babies were born and that he had a book about it, but he couldn't find it any more. Maytal believed everything he said and she loved him. She decided she would take good care of him by letting him be who he wanted to be: a smart little man.

Those springs and summers, Anezka took the three of them, Jakub, Maytal and Dana, Jakub's just born sister, to the cemetery in the Josefov. They were there almost every day. Anezka pushed Dana in the stroller up and down the alleys, and Jakub and Maytal roamed around the cemetery freely, avoiding other kids. They hid in faraway corners behind the tombstones and the old trees. They played house and school. Between cooking grass and pebbles and alephbet lectures, they kissed each other's hands and cheeks, whispering: "And I found out one thing: I love you", replying quickly with: "Gee Whiz!" as they saw it in the movies. They scratched into the cemetery wall their names, they read the just gilded and long faded words on tombstones. Jakub's voice was soft and his Hebrew was pleasant to listen to, so Maytal always let him read.

The Aunt's boy had the same aura of seriousness Jakub did. Only that seriousness, as his tomfooleries, if they could be called that, required a stringent bravery and physical skill. Although she always expected his instincts, his seemingly inborn knowledge about nature, the world, to take and keep control over any circumstance, she never ceased to be surprised and amazed by his readiness and courage. It seemed to Maytal the boy knew everything and that he knew her the best. He knew her limits and he never let her feel that she was left behind even a notch in any chore, in any running across the fields, any climbing up tall trees. He, without a doubtful mind, anticipated her cravings, appetites, yearnings and he readily provided for her.

Maytal couldn't eat the candy cane. She took ill that afternoon. The grease was washed off now and she slowly, painfully, stood up. The boy helped her walk back to the house. Soon the Aunt came running across the yard. She ordered the boy to boil plum brandy on the stove and to bring in more chopped wood. As he stepped out, the Aunt, without saying much, undressed Maytal to her bare skin and rubbed over Maytal's chest a comforting ointment. Then she dressed her in a sleeping gown and put her in the bed in the kitchen. She soaked a cloth in the boiling brandy and she put it on Maytal's chest and throat. On Maytal's feet she put another cloth soaked in the cooked tomato from the preserves, cold and soothing. She threw over Maytal a blanket and a heavy goose feather duvet. The boy brought in an armful of chopped wood and he surrendered to the stove two biggest pieces right away.

He and his mother sat to eat. The table was appropriately adorned with white china with a fine gold line on the edges. A delicate vessel, from a different set, filled with shredded horseradish stood in the center by an oval dish, once part of yet another set. It was topped with a heap of meat nicely cut in small cubes.

The two of them ate slowly, watching Maytal, breaking the feast to change the compresses with the brandy and tomato. After the meal, the Aunt and her son readied themselves for the church. The commotion and the cold air from the bedroom woke up Maytal from her feverish sleep. She opened her eyes and she saw the Aunt standing above her. The Aunt took the necklace off of her neck and she put the pendant, the circle like smooth, light colored stone, in a jar on the chair by Maytal's head. The jar was filled with water and floating marshmallow pieces. She whispered quickly and ominously over Maytal and the submerged pendant. The boy lowered the wick in the kerosene lamp. He put more wood in the stove and the two of them rushed to the church, as the night was falling.

Under Maytal's feet wrapped in tomato, in front of the window stood the Christmas tree. She saw it as an avalanche of candy canes and sparkles of reds, blues and greens coming in the kitchen together with the snow and night sky. The picture was well defined, the shapes and the colors seemed to be outlined, separated by a black thread, and Maytal thought she could see and count every snowflake against the blue backdrop. She wondered why the snow was not falling on the Christmas tree and her.

A gust of wind blew against the window and door, pushing in a whiff of familiar scent of cold, vast and deep water. Its surface was just about to freeze and become a deadly obstacle between the mouth and the skies above. This thought roused Maytal and she took a deep, sudden breath in her aching lungs. She sat up in the bed and looked around. On the chair by the headrest was the submerged pendant:

"Lilith," Maytal said.

On its flat, smooth and bright surface, veined with reds and blacks, were still lingering air bubbles that could not escape. Maytal reached for it. The stone dried quickly in her hand. A thin lace made of pelt went through the channel, skillfully drilled between the faces, paralleling the radius. Its surface appeared to be changing and Maytal put it closer to her eyes. The red and black veins started to gather under the dimmed light and the fire's glow, propping up themselves, resembling a human figure, an ox head, a house, a tree… Then the lines formed a spiral, starting from the edge, twirling toward the center, changing their colors into color of gold, writing fine, intricate letters. Maytal read: *vav, aleph, shin, resh, aleph… aleph, yod, beth*… Behind the letters, behind the whole surface, shone a stream of light and Maytal felt as if she was again in her back yard, listening to the voices and sounds coming from the kitchen. Her view was framed with the same eye orbits, so it wasn't hard to see everything she could remember. The four of them, her mother, father, Zayde, and she, were sitting on their stone threshold, which was now bright, and heavy, and hot, just as this stone was.

The fire reddened the stovetop, dancing under it and through the cracks, and it threw its blush on the walls and on the ceiling, now giving more light to the kitchen than the kerosene lamp. Maytal wanted to follow the light and the shadows, swayed by her own belief that she could see behind the shadows more than she could see on the Lilith's stone. And, yes, when she looked back at the stone, disenchanted and in panic, everything was already gone. Her eyes hurt, burning from their own, inner fire, and she closed them tightly, squeezing tears out and into the sweaty lump of her hair. She reached for the water and marsh mellow and she drank it in one gulp. She put the stone back into the empty jar and then slowly drifted away into a dreamless sleep, knowing now that she was alone.

The boy fed Maytal with soup filled with garlic and onions, with carrots and potatoes and beef marrow. He steeped tea for her at least twice a day, a strong, healing tea. With the tea, Maytal had to manage a thick slice of white bread topped with a glistening layer of wild strawberry jam. The boy was crafty, he knew everything. He was the one who cooked the soup and made the bread. She watched him subtly, hiding her smile. By the New Year, she recovered, convinced it was due to the boy's nurture and the stone in the jar.

Maytal quickly built up enough stamina to carry on with the boy. One Sunday, early in the day, they went further than usual. The boy kept this place as his secret. They took the main road, walking carelessly by the German's ramp, but no one stopped them. After a half hour of a good walk, they reached the sharp slopes by the half frozen creek. The hill was steep, almost vertical, exposed to sun and cold winds which turned the snow into a sheet of ice. As soon as they arrived, the boy threw himself on their small sled, head forward, and without a second thought, he pushed off his body over the edge. Maytal watched him with horror: he traded seemingly everything for the thrill of falling against the long wall of the icy abyss. He maneuvered digging his boots in the ice, leaning to one or the other side. The sled flew and within seconds it was at foot length away from the icy water. After his third flight, he said to Maytal they would go down by the orchard where it was much safer. But Maytal, not saying anything, let herself fall on the narrow sled, pushing it at the same time, going over the edge quickly, without hesitation.

It seemed like eternity. She didn't expect that she would need so much strength just to hold on to the sled. Her body shook and jumped and hurt. She found herself suspended in unusual silence, as if sound stayed behind her. Only the ice whispered under and in front of her. If it wasn't for those whispered words, the words of comfort, she would be left to herself, abandoned, she thought. A vague, uncertain feeling of anger grew deep inside her, in her fast beating heart and she wasn't frightened anymore. She let her grip loosen and her spirit rose right up, high, above everything. She saw herself below, rushing toward her destiny without anyone close enough to help her. The sled hit a small groove, it turned to one side and she was thrown off toward the creek's edge. She let herself roll and tumble, stopping only few inches of the perils of sharp rocks and freezing brook. She stayed on her back, beat up and tired. The boy let himself slide down, falling over his side once. He stood above her, his cheek and lip cut, bleeding, not knowing what to do. Maytal smiled at him. She had never seen him scared before. She started to chant, still on her back, in half voice, without a distinctive melody:

> *... Shlof shoyn mayn faygele*
> *Makh shoyn tsu dayn aygele*
> *Ikh bin shoyn meed atsind, lu, lu*
> *Shlof, shlof shoyn*
> *Shlof hob ikh dir gezoogt berele*
> *Ai, li li, lu lu...* [4]

The years went by. People were talking about the war's end. And there were days where one could think that it had really ended, if it wasn't for the Germans coming and going, patrolling, digging in, rounding up men and women to no apparent aim. One time the boy was summoned, together with a group of old men, to dig tranches on the hill by the brook. He had to dig still frozen earth for one whole week, and then he was let go. He said to Maytal that an officer asked him if he wanted to join the army. He answered that he had to ask his mother. The officer laughed and didn't bother him again.

Yes, the years passed and little Maytal grew. The Aunt made a burlap robe for her, tailored for a pregnant woman. She also made a small pillow with straps and Maytal had to tie the pillow under the burlap robe every time she went outside. She also had to dirty her hands and her face with soot and

---

4   From "Sleep in Sweet Repose", an old Yiddish lullaby

to smear her hair with kerosene. It was such a time and the Aunt worried. Then, the Germans were on the move and within a week most of them were gone. They left only a few of their men behind, just enough to oversee the train station and the four ends of the two roads. Now and then machinegun fire could be heard. It was coming from afar.

One sunny and warm Sunday that spring, the trees just started to overtake the dale with their modest bloom and mellow fragrance, Maytal walked to the edge of the woods, to the meeting spot. She was no longer wearing soot and the burlap robe. She was now clean and beautiful. She wore a simple dark blue coat, short and tight, and a linen skirt of the same color. Her long hazel hair was held back in a braid. Her bare feet stepped without hesitation over wet, cold grass. As she grabbed forward, her strong thighs showed under the fine linen. Over her arm, she carried a wicker basket with a knife in it. But when she arrived, she simply sat at the edge of the woods, looking down the road, away from the village. She sat there for a while without a thought in her head. The trees rustled and the birds flew and sang, a bee landed in her lap, the rare clouds travelled slowly across the clear and elusive bright blue.

Maytal lay down with her eyes opened and the blue veneer pulled back, shifted and caved. She felt its draw, but this time she looked back at it and at its pretence straight into the eye. This veneer of light and life and the cold and black chasm lurking behind couldn't scare her anymore. Her body felt stronger and heavier. She looked at the sky until it flattened, then she turned her eyes toward the sparrows in their short flights, toward the dandelion close by her face. She overgrew herself, she thought. The self that had to be suddenly and crudely uprooted and renamed, only to be hidden out of the view. And whose view? To whom she could have been such an eyesore? And to whom could her name be so hard on their ears, so it had to be hidden too. Quickly and impatiently she unbraided her hair and she took her clothes off. Then she lay back, now with the cold and green scent of grass and flowers against her white, young skin. She repeated to herself with whisper: "*Ikh bin Maytal*," in Yiddish.

The sunrays reflected off her whiteness and the spring breeze lingered over every hair and pore on her young body, making it feel cold and warm at the same time. She stayed lying like that for a long while. When a shadow from a tree fell over her, she put the clothes back on. She sat there for another minute with her arms over her knees, looking down the road, toward the village, and for the first time she felt she wanted to be somewhere else.

When she arrived, dinner was already set on the table. The Aunt and the boy waited for her with patience.

I came uninvited. I simply showed up at his door, making myself believe I came to see him only for my own reasons. Indeed, Maytal didn't ask me to do anything. Yet, it was obvious that she needed some things to be cleared up. Perhaps once and forever.

I don't want to mention his real name. Instead, I'll use one of many names he gave himself in the stories he wrote as a young man: Sam. And about his last name I will only say that it was serbianized sometime after the Balkan wars and then returned back into its original Yiddish by Sam's father, right after the family immigrated to Canada via Great Britain, just before WWII.

Sam spoke with nasal softness and, being wordy, his eloquence had plenty of strange syntax and rich vocabulary of perhaps questionable precision. On those rare occasions when we talked one on one, I would speak rarely and my few words would come out always being too solemn. He wanted every conversation to lead to a philosophical discourse, so I tried my best. But those of my best words were still without enough substantiation, always open for his interpretation and, I am sure, ridicule. His numerous points of view were unavoidably dogmatic and often incoherent and, in all honesty, there was nothing for me to say. So, I sat quietly before his arguments.

His words seemed to come out with great ease, almost by chance. Yet, at the same time there was always an expression of a struggle on his face, as the words formed on his tongue against his will. Also, over the years his persona adopted the Hebrew syntax and sentence intonation, as well as the guttural "k", and he would switch it on here and there, as if he was to remind me, and perhaps himself even more, that everything he said came from old Jewish wisdom. Although I pretended that there was an intention to talk only about consequential matter, I doubt now, as I did then, that Sam didn't know it was only loaded prattle that couldn't matter to anyone. When I think about it, it all looked like a dress rehearsal.

Sam had been back in Toronto for a sixth month now, after twenty-two years of his partial absence, the time he mostly spent between Tel-Aviv, Jerusalem, Washington D.C. and Toronto. After the usual pleasantries and a weak hug and a pat on the back we exchanged, this was the first he told me, as we walked into the sitting room:

"His wife asked him to put the pot with the leftovers in the fridge after we were done with it, and it turned out that the knob on the lid was too high for the shelf. So, he takes out all the things from the refrigerator to empty the shelf: eggs, meat, milk, rotten lettuce, dried up oatmeal, and then he moves the empty shelf up. Then he puts the pot and everything else back in, even the oatmeal. I ask in honest disbelief why he simply didn't flip the lid on the pot, and he gets all upset. Didn't I have some rights? What was I supposed to say? Or do? Well, all that turned into a big argument and I had to leave."

"So, there, so much for the brains of the head of MFI[5]. His monthly engagement would cost you fifty thousand, may be even more, American dollars, just to get a few pieces of advice from him and to have him fire one or two big shots of yours that you've gotten tired of overpaying. I stopped seeing him after that. Such an ignominy, and when you expect it the least."

He continued:

"Everyone is trying to carry himself on the back of old glory. That is repulsive. Revulsion is what I feel lately the most. And every day a bit more. People. The carelessness, the inconsiderateness, even toward themselves, actually mostly toward themselves, the negligence for their own thoughts and wishes, their blunt need for so called comfort which comes from militant ignorance and want-to-be-somebody-some-day laziness, those are their regular ways of living life and I am disgusted to the point that I cannot be among them anymore."

"The other day, I was invited to that place, up on Bathurst, to eat and to arrange my next trip, but I couldn't do it. First of all I could not eat there. Perhaps because the waiter reminded me of my father[6], perhaps because the bagel was stale, I don't know. Then I asked the boy, some schmuck they sent with the paper, a very simple question, for small talk's sake, trying to relax him, but he starts to lecture me. I made myself put some broth in my mouth, I signed the papers and excused myself. I ran out like a fury. Like a mad man. Now I am reconsidering getting Maytal back on board. I should have never agreed with her plans in the first place."

Maytal had taken care of his Toronto business for all those years. Her office was a smelly, over-furnished room, rich with artifacts and antique furniture, a room at the back of a house accommodating a small store at the front and three tenants upstairs. Sam worried about her health and he prohibited her from working there, he said. He was going to be looking for a nicer place soon, he promised.

"She started to be somehow careless, I worry about her. Can she change and not to be so stubborn? As if we can change at all? We are all now naturally at our worst and lowest, being close enough to the ultimate defeat, so don't you be making a mistake thinking that I am not taking seriously the natural order of things. Of course I am and because of it, I am working really hard on my flexibility. Of course I want her back, you must see it too: she

---

5   False acronym. Any match is coincidental.
6   Sam's father passed away many years ago.

and I were in so many ways and for so many years inseparable. But I need more time to work on my pliantness."

The concierge announced the hotel kitchen delivery. Sam had opened the door for them in advance. When they, two older men dressed in white, with boxes of food in their hands, showed up, he directed them toward the kitchen with a nod of his head. When they left, Sam went to the kitchen to inspect the food. He came back chewing and he sat further away from me. He put his feet on the coffee table, looking straight into my eyes. He offered me fresh figs from a heavy, dark green glass bowl on the table:

"I personally know the chef over there. She is very beautiful, very. Simply exquisite. And so young too. If you saw her on the street, you would never guess she was a chef. You'd think she was a model, or an actress. That's what I thought when I saw her for the first time, despite even her chef's hat. Perhaps you should meet her. You have an extremely weak spot for beautiful women, don't you? And strange ways about it, don't you? Come, let us eat. I didn't know you were coming, but there is plenty, and it's all kosher. We'll eat kosher today, we deserve it. Let us eat."

He called me to the table, but he stayed reclining in the rich black leather armchair, with his feet on the old green coffee table, close by the bowl with figs, perhaps waiting for me to get up first. His feet were in dark red socks with discrete yellow stripes, purchased probably somewhere in Europe earlier that year. They smelled of new shoes and pedicure talcum and I caught them touching the figs in the bowl at least two times. Perhaps unintentionally. I took a fig from the other end of the bowl and stood up. He followed me to the kitchen.

During the dinner he started to tell me, as I expected he would, one of his tales. His stories were never plain, or a soft and general account of a simple life. They were weighty, pretentious, with a, even for Sam, hard to reach meaning, or a point, or morals. They were hidden clumsily, and I suspect most of the time unintentionally, behind metaphors and parables, long pauses (due to inner, mental detours) and long, almost inciting staring looks. Also they, the stories, always ended abruptly. As if the storyteller suddenly became bored with it, or as if he became discouraged with the listener:

"About twenty years ago I was in Al Karak, to pay respects to my friend who was of my age, but who was torn apart very early in his life, so he died early.

It was that time when you simply wouldn't dare to cross the border on an Israeli passport, or British, or Russian for that matter, even to Jordan. I got in without the smallest problem thanks to family connections. I was irrecoverably late, two weeks or more, for the funeral. When I arrived to the house in Al Karak and, mind you, no one could have known of my presence there but the closest relatives of my departed friend, I was promptly sat to eat and then swiftly driven to the cemetery. My friend's brother-in-law was the driver. With us came along Jusuf, an Israeli, who lived in the house as a guest and a family friend. He was a writer, a poet etc., of Christian parents, but himself an atheist and an interesting fellow over all. In matter of fact, he might be living here, in Toronto, as we speak. Well, on our way to the cemetery, he tells me this story:

Ahmed

We lived in Hebron. My mother still lives there. I was only eleven then. And all what I wanted was a wristwatch I saw in the store a young Jew from Odessa ran. The store was primarily selling books. Books in Hebrew, Arabic, Russian and English. Also, there were candelabras, tablecloths, yarmulkes and candles. In the midst of all of this, there were seven wristwatches lined up on black plush in a small vitrine. One of them had to be mine.

The wristwatch I envisioned turned into an obsession. I coveted openly, I made my mother angry and worried. One week before school was to start, my father woke me up early and we left the house without breakfast.

We walked quickly and quietly. My heart was beating fast, my palms were sweaty: I knew we were going to buy the watch. My father bought it without much fuss. He didn't even want to haggle, the Jew gave us a break on his own. So, finally I had it. It was a Russian little beauty called 'Pobeda', meaning 'Victory', with three rubies in it, with a brown leather strap. Another man in the store, an old man, made a new hole in the strap for me and I left the store with the watch on my wrist.

I told you this in some detail and I didn't have to. It is important that you know I was only eleven and that I had a wristwatch. All this because the other boy was also eleven and he also had a wristwatch. His name was Ahmed and the watch he had was his father's. His father perished at sea, earlier that summer. Once Ahmed saw the watch on my wrist, he felt we shared the same destiny, as we did, of course, as we all do in the end, so he and I started to walk to school together.

The day before the Feast of the Exaltation, Ahmed told me his secret: ever since he had inherited the watch from his father, he started to run out of time. I didn't understand it at first, so we began timing our walk to school and from school, and every time it would take us, according to Ahmed's watch, more time to travel the same road. At the beginning of the school year we started with twenty three minutes, before the school break we were up to thirty, he said. I didn't believe him, of course. The next morning, it was Sunday, we woke up very early and we walked to the closed school. I measured the time on my watch and he measured it on his. My 'Pobeda' showed the usual twenty minutes, while his father's watch showed that four hours had irrecoverably elapsed. On our way back we walked very fast. My watch showed fourteen minutes had passed, his father's watch showed again four lost hours. We were both scared, but Ahmed made me swear not to tell anyone. I begged him to take his father's wristwatch off. He wouldn't listen. He missed his father too much. Before the school year ended, Ahmed needed a whole twenty-four hours just to arrive to school. Then another twenty four to go back home. The last time I saw him it was two days before the school year ended. And then, he was nowhere to be found. Ahmed simply disappeared.

Our friend here is under this heavy dirt too, under this cross. The Castles, the sea, the skies, you and I, we are now hidden from him. It may be forever or just for some short time. Who is to say?"

We had portabella mushroom soup, smoked salmon, beef roast covered with white sauce I could swear had cheese in it, more fish in yet another white sauce, challah, red Macedonian wine from his wine rack, which name Sam pronounced very naturally: Kratoshiya.

"I stayed in Al Karak for another couple of days, waiting for one of my friends' cousins to take his border guard shift. Jusuf never left my side for those couple days. He kept me awake telling me stories about our buried friend. And it turned out I didn't know about my friend as much as I thought I did. And I took it hard. I didn't know even that my friend wrote, that he wrote poems, stories, novels. That he was published and translated. I showed my disappointment with myself through subtle intolerance toward Jusuf. And, of course, Jusuf sensed it. Still, he wasn't giving up on his kind ways. It was an instance of transcendental friendship that I rejected because of the narrowness of my heart.

I was simply impotent to reciprocate even a morsel of any emotion I was offered so kindly and generously by Jusuf and by my mourning hosts. It was embarrassing, to say at least. And it bothered me big time. So, I tried to hide my shame behind my tiredness and a kind of absentmindedness I thought belonged to a man of my trade and status. Estrangement, that's what it was. I felt it then and there for the first time. And now I know it is imposed on me all over."

Maytal talked about Sam often. She wasn't hiding that she missed him. She talked about him as if he just stepped out for a moment, but was held somewhere for some unexplainable reason, for way too long, and now his dinner was getting cold. Sam never understood this. Sometimes, Sam would spend a week or two in Toronto, between his trips, and more than often Maytal and I learned about it only after he was already gone. It made us feel forgotten. And I knew not to look for Maytal then. I knew she needed time to mend herself: a week, two weeks, a month. Then she would find me and we would never mention what had just happened.

This time Sam was here to stay. At least that was what he said and that was how he acted. He has had his smaller apartment redone and he moved in only recently. That was why he hadn't contacted me for all this time, he said. And I believed him. In his apartment everything looked modern, shiny and new. Both bedrooms were done in a Japanese style, with black lacquer over hardwood floor, with Shoji closet doors decorated with Van Gogh drawings, with large and comfortable mattresses on the floor. The bathrooms were clearly European: the one which was part of the biggest bedroom was done in mosaic depicting "The Banishment from Paradise", after Masaccio's fresco, the other was simply tiled with pink Tuscany marble. The sinks, toilets and bidets were made of forged copper, of a modern, elegant design.

The dining room was big enough to accommodate a large walnut dining table and eight chairs with alizarin red seats, one heavy crystal chandelier, precariously hanging above the walnut, and a walnut china cabinet. The chandelier and the cabinet Sam inherited from his mother. The table and chairs were custom made some time ago to match the cabinet.

The sitting room, as Sam called it, was the biggest room in the apartment. The scarce furniture made it look even bigger. By the plantation shutters made of cherry wood, stood a red lacquered liquor cabinet set on an angle against the corner. Once it had been a linen armoire Sam had me redesign and make into a liquor cabinet. A substantial black leather sectional and an old "Heintzman" grand piano, matte black, with a giant silver menorah on it, dominated that part of the room. Toward the entrance on the wall, between the old oils (the oils I've already seen before) depicting Israeli landscapes, there was no new art. And none of my paintings hanged there. They were still in Tel-Aviv, Sam said. He continued with the discourse:

"We are insignificant paradigms firmly believing in all sorts of fairytales. Yes, we got our lives, our time, but how does it matter, what does it measure against? What is the reference point? There is none I can see. Our time, it doesn't measure against anything, so we can say we don't have even that. We have nothing really. There is nothing for us here, out there, anywhere. We, humanity, we are suspended in eternity like a dead monster: motionless, ugly, frightening and frightened. Some see it, some don't. Some believe it, some are hopeful. Hopeful for what? How can I be hopeful? We are in a lose-lose situation! And there is nothing we can do about it. We are helpless and the Cosmos is indifferent. And I tell you, it is much more indifferent than it is chaotic. No help is coming ever. It will be like all this has never happened. What am I saying? It is already like nothing had happened. All these words, days and nights, dreams, murders, betrayals, love, lips and eyes we sing about, gods, everything, all this in the end falls back into universal indifference, where definitions don't exist. There the noblest heart is the same as a bad dream, or a rotten tooth in the head of a dying cat."

I stumbled on Sam's poems, the beginning of a novel (two chapters) and on his half-baked philosophical essays and notes he wrote as a student.

I bought from him a typewriter, together with two boxes of paper, one opened and the other untouched. I got it just before he moved to Haifa, it was a long time ago. And in the opened box under the clean paper I found the Sam's writings and I read all of it that same night.

Sam took Political Sciences and Jewish Philosophy when he was thirty-three, hoping to put between himself and his bank managerial job a high and thick wall of esotery that philosophy of politics, or philosophy itself, he thought, routinely assembles.

He wrote:

"As much as one who reads Ben Petura's and Rabbi Akiva's conundrum understands the need not to see the ill logic in Ben Petura's proposition, therefore in its outcome, there is still one. My wish is to expose it, but not to condemn it. I want to show the ill logic, so I can round Ben Patura's proposition as infinitely irrational and as such transpose it into an allegory of infinite love, hence an utopia, that, in my opinion, led toward the spine of the idea of early Christianity, and such to contrast it against today's averaged concoction of liberal democracy and cynicism of the world(s).

I suggest that the beginning of the problem with Ben Petura's proposition can be found in the demands of the Halakha: one must not commit murder (passively or actively) in order to save his own life. *Rashi's comments in the Sanhedrin imply that the obligation to save one's own life DOES NOT EXIST AT ALL if he is given the choice between sacrificing his own life and taking the life of another. He writes, "The King's word cannot be pushed aside, for he commanded against murder."* (R. E. Krumbein).

I will agree for now with this Rashi's, i.e. Ben Petura's comment and make of it my ethical pivot. This is to say that I temporarily disagree with Rabbi Akiva's "*Ve-chai achikhaimakh," - your life takes precedence* (ib.) concept."

And it continues like this on fifteen pages, only to prove, to himself in the end, that Rabbi Akiva's ethics should always prevail.

Or:

"One who thinks abstractly will find himself isolated from the world which is nothing else but a conglomerate of former abstractions. This proves the young, narcistic age of humanity."

Or:

"The idea of progress is anthropocentric. A part cannot progress by itself. For the whole cannot be said to have progressed because of the inherited absence of a reference point. Therefore, humanity cannot progress by itself. The illusion of progress is caused by changes in paradigm, by the sense of directional time and space."

Or:

"We are all potentially equipped with everything necessary to be a reliable witness. Is this the purpose? To be the observer of creation?"

Above an unfinished novel's (two chapters) title ("Conversion"), there is the name of E.M. Narretho, obviously a pseudonym, (deciphered it spells 'other name', plus a superfluous 'r'). I always wondered why Sam wanted to conceal the author's name. It was well written, with the right measure of wordiness and with the sentiment of a worldly man. I never mentioned those two chapters to him and he never asked.

And at the very bottom of the box I found fifty-three poems. They were written for the World. They were didactic and anachronous and for a long time I kept them as a reference, a point of origin of Sam's ideals.

Sam continues in the sitting room:

"Such ordinary things to talk about. It seems there is nothing else."

We sat in silence for a while. When it became apparent we would snooze off, he said:

"But for now, we have a responsibility to maintain the world. Here, take another fig. And let us get some more goodness in our bodies. This is the kind you like."

He took from the red lacquered cabinet two crystal shot glasses and a bottle shaped like The Wheel of the Chariot, with the familiar golden and blue label, with arching Cyrillic letters reading: *"Šljivovica"*. He poured the glasses, spilling the heavy and greasy liquid on the dark green surface.

"L'chaim. To Ahmed."

We drank it all at once. As soon as we empted the glasses, he filled them again, this time not spilling a drop.

We drank now sipping it in silence, taking it only on our lips, feeling the plum, barrel and the soft fire it was once baked on. The slits on the shutters darkened and I tried to guess the hour. Sam fell back on the couch with his eyes closed. He said:

"I don't want you to leave. Unless you must, of course. But even if you must, please stay."

"I need few minutes like this," he said. "Only few minutes. I have been up and around since five. Had to call Tel-Aviv, but I missed the time. Slept one minute too long, I guess."

"I promised myself this would be my last honorarium. At least for some time. One has to be also realistic."

He lay down, quiet, his face gray. Tiredness came over me too. I felt it first on my head, then it travelled down my chest and limbs. The room started to sink into silence and darkness. But then, at once, Sam sat up and flicked the switch on the long floor lamp made only of thick, frosted glass. The lamp stood behind him, in the corner between the sofa and the wall, its light spilling only inches away from the thick glass, as if it couldn't quite escape. It turned Sam into a silhouette of a fragile, imperfect and old man. I wanted to move, to change my viewpoint, and I sat closer to the coffee table. I reached for a fig.

"Please give me another five minutes. It must be the brandy. It hit me straight in the head. Just five minutes," Sam said.

He again slumped in the black leather and he closed his eyes. I saw his face getting grayer and older under the diffused, soft glow. His mouth opened a bit and he started to snore, quietly and with interruptions. His right foot was still on the floor and it was bothering him, but he didn't have control over it anymore. I closed my eyes and leaned my head against the headrest, still chewing the fig, trying to stay awake. I held myself like that for some time, but then, with the sweetness in my mouth, my head slumped toward my chest and my whole body slowly slid down.

As I looked across the dark green surface at Sam, I understood I would never have courage to mention Maytal to him. The time had passed and nothing could be changed anyway. She hid from me her disappointments, her thorn inside, her tired heart, her sickness for a long time. It enraged me and I wanted to tell her that now I was a different man. Less and more of everything. A changed man who will claim his own from now on. I looked for her down a hallway, and she was already at the door knocking. Sam rushed toward to greet her, but when she saw me, she ran down the stairs. I ran after her as she walked toward her car. She turned toward me, asking about my indifference. I said I had none. I said I was a changed man.

We drove up the winding and steep road leading toward the farmland and villages, then down through the villages and small townships, and further down by the patches of woods and pastures. We drove for hours, neither of us not saying a word, until the dusk started to cut across the fields and around the trees. I found myself in darkness. A woman's voice spoke in a distance, softly, as if it was reading a fairytale, and at once I understood it was Maytal's voice. I called for her, only to quiet the voice into absolute silence.

Sam covered me with a blanket and it woke me up. But a feeling of abashment came over me and I pretended to be still asleep. I heard him walk away, then I heard him in the kitchen. I waited a bit and, when I felt the smell of toasted bread, I sat up, pushing the blanket away.

"Come over here. I am making sandwiches and tea," Sam said from the kitchen.

The clock on the stove was showing eleven thirty. Sam smeared cream cheese on toasted bread and now he was putting thin slices of smoked salmon on it. The gray hue on his face has disappeared. He looked rested and hungry and ready to tell me another story.

But after the salmon and the strawberry tea, Sam decided it was more fitting to listen to a jazz record. We listened. Sam would say a word or two about the music, struggling to find the right ones. Soon the gray hue came back on his face again and he quieted down. The tiredness that came over me this time was heavier and darker, like punishment. I didn't want Sam to see me fall asleep, so I tried to follow the rhythm from the record with the tips of my fingers against my knee. But when the music stopped, I realized that I had already been asleep. The blanket was over me again and Sam was in his bedroom, snoring quietly. I turned over onto my side and I put my hand between the leather cushions. They were cold and soothing.

At first I started to fall, to tremble, then I felt ground under my feet. I wanted to find the place where Maytal left me. I strained to see through the thick night, sabotaged and tricked and broken. Oh, Maytal, I haven't changed, I know I haven't. I know this desolate space too well, I whispered. Then I fell into a dreamless sleep, defeated.

Sam woke me up. He called my name. I turned on the light in his bedroom. He was lying on his side, covered up to his eyes. His voice came under the silk comforter, dampened and weak:

"Call an ambulance. Actually, call Max first. My address book is on the big desk. The big black book on my desk. His home number. He must be in his bed now. Dr. L., but you'll find him under 'M.'"

Dr. L. wasn't answering. I called the ambulance and then I called Dr. L. a few more times, but to no avail. I stayed in the sitting room at the big desk. Sam was quiet. The paramedics finally arrived. They were led to the apartment by the doorman. They banged on the door forcefully. It was two of them and they worked very quickly. They immediately put the oxygen tubes in Sam's nostrils and without much effort they lifted him onto the stretcher. Then they quickly pushed him into the elevator. Sam was scared. He looked lost, small. Yet he said:

"Please, stay behind. The keys are in the tray on the commode. Don't forget to lock the dead bolt too if you must leave. And don't let Maytal know about this. I am very sick, very. I don't want her to worry. You don't worry either. Don't forget the dead bolt."

The elevator door closed. I went back to the apartment. The sun had risen in the mean time: the bedroom at the end of the long hallway was bathing

in light. I found the keys and I left. That evening, I went to the hospital to
see Sam.

My mother died in that same hospital more than twenty years ago and I
still remembered the layout. I came in through the main entrance. Down the
hall I knew to expect the morgue. Past the morgue were four elevators and
the stairwell. I took the stairs.

That autumn I had my first exhibition. The hospital called me at the
gallery. A young girl, part time help at the gallery office, took the call. She
left the handset by the phone on the table for me.

A nurse handed me my mother's belongings: the old, worn clothes and
shoes, two oranges and the catalog, the four black and white pages I had
printed at my own expense and which I brought for her the day before. They
were crumbled and torn. She rolled over it in her nightmares of pain and
expiring breaths, I thought. The hearse came with a coffin already at the
back, a simple light brown coffin. I sat by the driver, quiet, with the white
plastic bag in my lap and we drove to the cemetery morgue.

The unstoppable drizzle, which started in September and rolled over to
October that year, was steadily adding, with its coldness and its grayness,
another dimension of ache to bones and souls. Beside the Rabbi, the grave-
digger and me, there were three more people at my mother's burial. Those
three boys and I used to do handyman work for the shul. We also used to
clean the shul kitchen and basement before Pesach. Later, the four of us
learned the carpentry trade together. My mother fed them and she washed
their clothes. They stood with me solemn, resolute to help. They offered to
sit *shiv'ah* with me, but I refused. I sat *shiv'ah* alone in the gallery among my
paintings and in my apartment, without the lights turned on.

Now, I was back in the hospital. Before I took the stairs, I hid my plastic
raincoat under a sink in one of the bathrooms.

I found Sam asleep on his back in a big and comfortable bed. The oxygen
tubes were still in his nostrils. I came close to him. On his forehead, cheeks
and neck were round red patches demarcated with white borders. His face
was tight, doll-like. He was struck by an infliction from which one recovers
only by a miracle, I thought. I sat in the armchair by the window and I looked
at his narrow rib cage under the fine blanket. At times his chest seemed to be
still, lifeless, but then it would expand, making a sound of undisturbed sleep
and convalescence. And I felt as if I were at his mercy more than I had ever
been before.

The drizzle had stopped, but the raindrops still lingered on the hospital
glass. The air was colored by the lights glimmering in the windows of the
apartments and offices, on the streets, on the rushing cars. The clocks every-
where turned unnoticeably but relentlessly yet another minute. I walked

out of Sam's room, down the endless corridors, down the stairs and onto the street.

I left Sam's apartment quickly after he was taken to the hospital, not locking the dead bolt. I sat on a tram that took me to Maytal's house, but Maytal was still not there. The kitchen light and the light in the small bedroom were lit. Maytal would leave them on if she planned to stay overnight in Hamilton. For safety reasons. I wrote a message for Maytal and stuck it in the door.

The sun already had warmed up the morning. I walked slowly up the street to the park and then I cut across grassy knolls and through the bush. The shortcut led to the parking at the back of my apartment building, but when I got there, instead of going upstairs, I turned right down the street, passed the gallery with two of my oil paintings in the window, passed the secondhand guitar store and I went into the coffee shop. The young woman behind the counter was sleepy and she moved around slowly. A man at the small table was having breakfast with his two large dogs.

I bought pastry with spinach and cheese and I ate it in the park, sitting against a big fir. Then I fell asleep resting my head on my arms over my knees. Some time later a policeman woke me up. He asked me if I was all right. I smiled and I made a remark about the beautiful day we were given to enjoy. He smiled back and he said that it might rain. I didn't disagree with him and we went our separate ways. I went to my apartment.

The street commotion and the breeze, smelling of rain and dust, woke me up from my dreamless sleep. The window glass, despite its layers of dirt, reflected reds and oranges into the room. I was hungry.

I knew I would have to look for Sam in one of the private rooms and I readied myself: I shaved and put a clean shirt on. I put on my raincoat, an inexpensive sheet of thin plastic, and I rushed out.

It was drizzling the leftovers of the rain I slept through. My paintings still stood in the gallery window. They've been sitting there for over a year now and so many times I thought to take them back. But every time I would bring myself to do it, Maytal talked me out of it.

This time the coffee shop was packed. The evening girl knew me. She gave me my sandwich and coffee without asking. I crossed the street to the park and I quickly nestled in, hidden from view and rain by an evergreen bush. After I ate my dinner, I sat utterly thoughtless, listening to the distant and vague sounds of the city getting ready for the night, drinking my coffee.

A group of hooligans showed up out of nowhere. They were coming my way, talking loudly, swaggering. I lay down on the bed of dry needles, holding my breath. They walked past me, swearing and laughing. I waited for them to disappear and, once I couldn't hear them anymore, I quickly cut toward the closest opening in the wrought iron fence. My tram was turning the corner. I jumped on it. It took me right to the front of Maytal's door. My note was still there as I had left it. I took it and I put it in the only pocket on my raincoat. Then I quickly walked down the street, toward the hospital.

I was eighteen, just having finished carpentry school, when my mother was diagnosed with cancer. It started to eat her stomach long before, but because it progressed too slowly, the doctors didn't see it coming. And when her stomach grew and hardened, when it spread to her lungs and liver, when the pain became impossible to bear, the doctor's diagnoses wasn't necessary anymore. The surgeon who opened my mother's stomach, only to declare the case hopeless, wondered about her endurance. He said she beat all the odds and he ordered for her to be kept in the hospital. My mother reacted as if the hospital bed and the impatience of overworked, tired nurses was the reward she hoped for all her life. And as soon as she lay down in the narrow bedstead of wet mattress, pain and morphine, she wanted me to sell our house and to use the money to stay in school. She insisted on it with an enthusiasm and conviction that come only from the euphoria of departing.

So, I sold the house to the shul, months after my mother passed away. They paid fair money for it. A young couple, converts, with three small children and one on the way, moved in. I took an apartment in the West End. By then, I had finished carpentry school and I had a job installing kitchen cabinets. And I surrendered my portfolio to the faculty of fine arts.

I went back to retrieve my raincoat the next day. It was lunch time when I arrived. A woman was cleaning the washroom in which I hid my raincoat. I decided to wait in the cafeteria. There, sitting by the tinted window, Sam was having lunch. He was in a hospital robe and he didn't look ill anymore. Across him was a man in a white coat. It was Dr. L.

I approached their table:

"A visit by a friend," Sam said when he saw me. "The timing couldn't be better. I am on my way out. I've just gotten flying colors. Did you bring my keys?"

I lied. I said I didn't have his keys on me. Sam quickly hid his disappointment. He said to the doctor:

"Max, this is my friend, an artist, a poet. A smart man."

Dr. L. smiled at me and immediately shook my hand. He shook Sam's hand too and then he hurriedly left. Sam said to me:

"Well, I am sorry if I gave you the scare. I gave it to myself too, the scare of my life. It turned out it was an allergy. They would like to see what I am allergic to, but I think I already know: it's this place, this city. Well, how are we going to get my keys now?"

In the taxi, on the way to my apartment, Sam, still in his hospital robe, said:

"Everyone thought it was my heart. Because of my age, I guess. Ha, ha, I thought that too. But, nothing is wrong with me, nothing. Perhaps this should scare me: in my age and nothing is wrong?"

I found in my mailbox a blue envelope with Maytal's handwriting on it. I sat in the atrium where Sam couldn't see me, and I opened the letter. On a sheet of paper ripped from a notebook, Maytal wrote:

"I hope you haven't already gone to him, but I know you have. I am still in Hamilton, in Saint Joseph's. I fell on the street. Come. Bring me something to change."

I sneaked toward the stairwell and I left the building through the superintendant's door. I ran across the parking and I quickly found myself in the park. I ran through the park toward the tram stop. The tram came just as I was catching my breath. I hopped on.

Maytal's house smelled of wreaths. There, by the kitchen sink, still wrapped in paper, lay two big bouquets of yellow and red roses. The radio played very quietly in the bedroom. I turned it off. I found a small traveler's bag in the closet, made of fine, tanned hide. Inside it were two worn man's shirts, socks and underwear and a handful of *agorot*, half-shekels and shekels. In the inside pocket were also a few five and ten shekel banknotes. I put the money in my pocket and I threw the leather bag back into the closet. I found a plastic bag in the kitchen, I put Maytal's few necessities in it and I rushed out. But, instead to Union Station, I went back to Sam's apartment.

The concierge, the man I knew for a long time, we knew each other from the carpentry shop where we used to work together, handed to me two envelopes for Sam. One had Maytal's handwriting on it.

I took the stairs. I forced myself to run up. I ran two flights before my lungs started to burn. On the last turn, my shirt caught on the handrail and ripped. The small pearl like buttons fell on the concrete landing. I sat down and opened the envelope with Maytal's handwriting:

I am held back unexpectedly and it is my fault. By the time I am done, you will be most likely back in Israel. I know this and I don't hold it against you. I stayed with you because I thought you needed me. Perhaps that's the worst thing that can happen to anybody. M.

Before I opened Sam's door, I put my ear against it. Then I walked in loudly, slamming the door behind me. I went straight to the red lacquered cabinet. The side further from the window had a hidden access to a deep, shelved compartment. It was for *mazzikin*, Sam said when he asked me to make it for him. I opened it easily. Inside on the shelves were a bundle of envelopes held together with an elastic band, one plush bag with tefillin and tallit, two round aluminium boxes with eight millimeter films, an old tin box from a bicycle tube repair kit, now filled up with gold and diamond tie pins and cuff buttons. On the topmost shelf were two small Siddur books, which covers were adorned with silver lace and rubies and emeralds. Sam put those Siddurs away not because of their value, but because of their pretentious character that he secretly liked. Beside these keepsakes, there were stacks of American and Canadian dollars, Deutsche marks and French francs. I took all that money. I put it in two blue shopping plastic bags with Hebrew and English letters on them that read: *Elal, Many Happy Returns*. Then I made a sandwich with cream cheese and salmon on a toasted bagel and I ate it there, sitting on the tall stool, my elbows on the Tuscany marble, taking small bites and chewing slowly, sipping cold water from a crystal wine glass.

"Are you Jakub", the nurse, a very young woman, asked me. I showed her my City Transport pass.

"She is over here," the nurse said coming out of the reception. She turned a few times toward me, making sure I followed her. In the morgue, as we were standing above Maytal's covered body, the nurse said:

" Is Jakub coming too?"

The knock on my door woke me up. I fell asleep waiting for it. The bags with the money stood by the door. And I wasn't sure if it was Sam all by himself, or if he came with the police. I called them in, but in my doorway stepped a telegram man. He stood there for a moment, then walked in. I stood by the window. He handed me his book to sign and then he gave me the telegram in the return for the book, as if we were trading.

I let Maytal wait, Maytal: quiet, covered, desperate, the telegram said.

Deborah started to cry and Avi put the Siddur down and sat by her. The usual Friday evening commotion, with an undertone of fast steps and a few Yiddish and Hebrew words being called out here and there, was coming in through the wide open kitchen window. It seemed everyone was going to the shul but the three of us. We already blessed the light, the challah and the wine. The Shabbat dinner was waiting. We sat at the table. I broke the challah.

I came for Maytal. I put my hand over her hands under the white cover and I felt the weight of her whole body.

Je to smeteno
Mé Rudé Prázdno
A nitro se třese
Zimou a v děse a ted
Skoro není kam jít
Hranou oka
Dny sečteny
Ve vysoké trávě blízícího léta
Pod nimi budeme položeni
Vyprahlí a bolestní
Jak rychlý ten obrat byl!
Ten pravní výkřik ještě daznívajíc
Stále přítomen a přec
Ten čas nic nedělání se dostavil

I wrote this poem for my Maytal, my little Marjeta, while she disapproved of my brooding ways. She often recited it to me, her lips close to my ear, close to my face, making her deep voice deeper, amorously distracted and lost between the memories, hers and mine, scorning me, telling me there could not be so much truth in words.

The day I put Maytal in her grave was just like this day: at a standstill yet wavering under this big Sun. Beside the Rabbi and me, no one else was there. Turtledoves called from behind motionless evergreens and ash, the wood in the tomb echoed its destiny under the clumps of earth. After he recited the Psalms and *El Maleh Rachamim*, the Rabbi offered me a ride:

"Let me help. Anything I can do," he said.

Deborah dries her tears and brings the tcholent from the kitchen. Avi is standing in the window and watches the passers by. I pour up the sweet wine in our goblets and the three of us sit at the table. Avi recites the blessings for the bread and wine again.

Many months later, I went to pick up the money for my paintings. A man purchased both of them, the gallery owner said over the phone. When I asked for the man's description, the gallery owner said he couldn't describe the man with any certainty. The most accurate thing one could say would be that he was out of place.

I went for the money just before closing time. The night was warm and pleasant, with familiar scents and sounds, seemingly coming always from afar. The gallery owner invited me for a drink and we walked up the street past my old place to a bar I had never seen before. We sat at a small, worn down table to drink wine.

The gallery owner wanted to tell me about his encounters with the customers who enjoyed one or the other sort of fame, and he kept talking decanter after decanter. I was quickly caught in the haze of the pomace bitterness and yeasted sweetness and I couldn't keep track of the names and events. In my role of a careful listener, I watched the tired waitresses sliding between the tables, the people coming in and leaving, trying to follow my interrupted thoughts. Then, a young woman came in. She stood at the door, scanning the room quickly. She was in a yellow, light dress, her dark hair was held tightly at the back, it made her look prettier than she was. She made her way to an empty table. When she sat down, the light fell on her face and at once I saw it more clearly, as if it suddenly came closer to mine. She looked back straight into my eyes and she smiled. I recognized Maytal and myself in that smile and I remembered my raincoat I left in the hospital.

I stumbled out on the street and started down, toward the park, toward the tram. A group of hooligans stood by the gate, swearing loudly at each other. I walked through them and a half of a cigarette hit my shoulder. I stopped. I felt them coming toward me, but I wasn't running away. I sat on the bench. They stood around, watching me without a word. Then someone said:

"Leave the shit. I know him. He's a cock sucker," and they all laughed.

"Fucking faggot," someone else said in a high pitched voice. They turned away from me. A few more lit cigarettes flew my way as they walked out through the gate, swearing loudly at each other again.

The raincoat was still tightly wrapped and hidden under the sink. It was a bit damaged by the hot water pipe. I put it under my arm and, quickly as I could, I walked out of the hospital.

I read the message under a shop window light:

And whoever holds the world's treasures does so however he came by them. It is otherwise in the world of spirit.

The money I took, I gave away. I gave it to charities, to pan handlers, to soup kitchens, to shelters.

I haven't changed anything in Maytal's house. The things from my apartment, the easels, the paints and brushes, the clean and painted canvases, I put in the attic.

And there, in the attic, between the brush strokes, I often stand by the tall and narrow window, with the bright stone in front of me on the window's ledge. Not too far from my watchtower is the rooftop of the house in which my mother and I once lived. It lies there with its wings spread, motionless, insipidly finding its reason to protect those under.

BEZZA

The last time we saw each other we were five years old. Now I am fifty-five and I am back home. Although I knew only his nickname, I had never stopped thinking of him as of my best friend. Yet, when I moved back into our old house, I didn't ask about him. Perhaps I thought there was no one to ask.

By the west corner of the old iron fence covered with white and pink rose bushes, there was a small gate leading into a narrow concrete yard, more of a passage, and at the end of it there was the coach house, turned into two small apartments during my long absence. One apartment was empty and in the other, I was told, lived the house handyman Theodore. I saw him once or twice from afar. He was a strong man in his early seventies, with a full head of silver hair, with broad shoulders and big hands. He also chauffeured my Bubbe on her errands.

I walked by him one day as he was digging out the mandrakes in front of the house. A tall heap of dark green, broad leaves and sullied torsos lay in the wheelbarrow. He said to me:

"Hi, Daniel. I am sure you don't remember me. I am Theodore."

"I know who you are. My Bubbee told me," I said.

"But I am sure you don't remember me from before. We met only once, just before I was sent to the front, just before you left for America. You were very little then. I am Christopher's brother."

"Christopher's brother?" I said. "Who is Christopher?"

"Bezza, my baby brother. He asked about you upon your return."

For a very long time I hadn't heard anyone say his nickname. Theodore said:

"You two were inseparable. Remember?"

"Sure I do. Where is Bezza now?"

"Bezza is at home", Theodore said and motioned toward the coach house, " but he is not well."

He reached under the mandrake leaves in the wheelbarrow and pulled out a bottle. It had four fingers of plum brandy in it. He took a sip:
"He isn't well at all, for a long time now. Not well at all," he said.
"What do you mean?"
Theodore lit up a cigarette:
"He sleeps all the time. Sixteen, twenty hours every day. And when he's awake, he does nothing. Just sits and stares."
"Did he see a doctor? What does the doctor say?"
"Doctor? Except for those couple months he spent in the House, he never wanted to see any doctor."
"Can I see him? When is he awake?"
Theodore took another taste of the brandy. The cigarette was burning between his fingers:
"The best bet is this Wednesday. Two men used to come to visit him almost every day, but now they come only on Wednesdays since I told them so. They've kept coming for the last twenty-something years. They sit and talk, make him company. Bezza says it's because of the book."
"The book?"
"He'll tell you and you'll see everything yourself, I am sure."
"Then I'll go to see him this Wednesday. But what time?"
"They come usually around three in the afternoon and then they sit and wait for him to wake up. I guess you will have to wait with them."
I went to see Bezza that Wednesday. I entered the concrete yard through the old iron gate. The summer shower washed the concrete that morning and now it was shiny and smelled clean.
The door was ajar and I walked in without knocking. The two men were already sitting on an old bench in the long hallway. They didn't say anything when I came in. I sat beside them. Soon after I sat, the door at the end of the hallway opened and the men stood up without delay and walked toward the door, still in silence. I followed them.
The room was dark and it smelled of rosemary. The only window in the room was covered with a colorless, thick curtain, but a streak of blue daylight found its way in. My eyes quickly adapted. The space opened slowly in front of me and I saw a long and narrow makeshift bed in the middle of the room. The two men took the chairs closer to the hunched silhouette on the edge of the bed. I didn't dare, or I didn't want to move. My pupils opened even more and now I could see even the golden embroidery on the linen sheet over Bezza's shoulders. When the men sat across him, he sat up tall. He turned toward me and I saw his long and unkempt hair was half covering his face. He turned quickly away from me, pushing the hair behind his ears. I heard his voice: quiet, deep and raspy, still needing time to wake up. He greeted the men with a long, vibrating sentence.

The gathering didn't take long. One hour at the most. Bezza spoke and the men nodded their heads, saying little. Then suddenly it was over. The men put the chairs back against the wall and then they left quickly and quietly. Bezza motioned to me to approach. I sat by him on the edge of the bed. Up close, his face was skinny and pale. It looked unearthly and unapproachable:

"Theodore told me you were not well. How are you doing, Bezza?"

He smiled at me:

"You left right after we took the rockers off of your wooden horse."

"I remember it. It was quite a feat."

"Yes," Bezza said, "quite a feat."

"Theodore also told me you wrote a book. I would love to read it."

"Theodore told you that? I didn't think he would ever mention it to anyone. He suffers and I am the reason. I know. You are a writer yourself, you should know: it is an unstoppable infliction. In my case, I probably brought it on myself. I opened my mind, so to speak."

He picked a half of an apple from the bowl on the small table by the headrest and took a small bite. Then he put the apple back into the bowl:

"I read all of your books. I keep them in the other room, on the shelf under the window. And about my book: well, my book has vanished. It has disappeared over night, unnoticeably, just after it was out."

"Vanished?"

"The manuscript and the printed copies, the plates."

"I don't understand," I said.

"Me neither," he said.

"The plates? That is incredible. So, you don't have even one copy?"

"I am telling you: like it never existed."

We sat quietly for a short while.

"Those two men, who are they?" I said.

"They used to work in the printing house. They were the typesetters. They want to recreate my book."

"You know your book by heart?"

"Of course not. I can tell if an idea was right or wrong, but only if I am asked in the right way. They know what and how to ask. They put it together already once, letter by letter."

"Why do you sleep this much?" I said. "If you didn't have to sleep this much, the book would be rewritten by now, wouldn't it?"

"All working men think I sleep too much. Are you a workingman too? I don't think you are. And I don't think I sleep too much. Anyhow, we are over the first half and it doesn't feel like it will take much longer."

"Twenty years just for the first half? How big was the book?"

"Twenty years? What do you mean by it?"

"The men have been coming for twenty years now, Theodore said."

"He said that? Can it be twenty years?"

"Can it be?"

"I want you to tell me: can it be twenty years?"

He was visibly upset. He stood up and quickly walked to the window. With one quick and decisive motion he removed the curtain. A bright picture opened itself in the wall. For a while I could see only his darkened silhouette against the brilliant screen. He said:

"But how could you be so sure if it is true? You were away. Yet, you say it very confidently: 'twenty years.'"

He turned toward the window:

"But look: the street hasn't changed at all. There is a hot summer afternoon and the heavens are red and green and purple and orange. And listen. Hear the turtledove: she coos from afar in her loneliness. Now hear the ringing of horseshoes against cobblestone and a squeak of wheels. They are coming toward us and…here it is."

A big, strong red horse passed through the window's frame, pulling a cart. I recognized our ice-delivery man sitting on it. He was now an old man and on the back of his cart he didn't carry ice blocks anymore.

"The ice-delivery man," I said.

Bezza watched the man on the cart turning down the street toward the river. Then he approached slowly and sat by me. I felt again heavy and immobile. We sat like this quietly. The window opening darkened in the mean time. Someone lit a light in the house across the street. Bezza lay down:

"I never stopped thinking of you as if you were my best friend," he said before he slowly fell into sleep.

I sat by him for a bit longer. Only the warm breeze and the turtledove disturbed the evening silence. On my way out I put my chair back by the wall.

Outside the iron gate I stood by the rose bush in its soft smell for some time, looking down the street, toward the downtown glow, toward the promenade. Then I slowly walked there.

SPINOZA

Joe, Rabbi Gold's only son, a big fellow, some ten years older than us, in his mid thirties, talked more than usual that Shabbat evening. He talked loudly and at length, he quoted long passages in Hebrew, and his small, beady and dark eyes were piercingly asking for the agreement of a rare listener.

"I have a hard time believing all those stories about him," Morris said to me on the way home. "At least his mother could tell him to change his shirt and pants from time to time. Every single fringe has some kind of food in it."

Joe was a *wunderkind*, the stories went, but Morris didn't hesitate to challenge Joe every time they met.

"Why are you so mean to him?" I asked.

"I don't know. Perhaps it's his hygiene, perhaps it's his fake antiquity, perhaps it's the way he talks, you pick. He just gets on my nerves."

A month later Morris and I decided to go to the shul for Shabbat again. We sang loudly and drummed hard on the sides of the pew, my palms and knuckles hurt. The women behind the *mekhitza* made of a white, lacey curtain looked at Morris and me and some of them smiled back at us.

That evening Joe was quiet during the prayers and before the service was over, he approached Morris:

"Morris, what do you have against me?" he asked quietly.

This surprised Morris, just as it surprised me. Finally Morris said:

"Daniel and I are going for a beer just about now. If you join us, I'll tell you why."

"Just about now? You know I cannot do that."

"Well, why not?"

"You know why."

"Because you are a Jew?"

"Yes. It's Shabbat. And you shouldn't go either."

"Jesus, Joe, lighten up. What is wrong with a glass of beer after a good Shabbat song?"

Joe looked sadly at Morris and smiled:

"Well, since you mentioned Jesus himself. Alright, Morris, I'll go. Any time you are ready."

When we stepped out from the shul, Morris and I took our yarmulkes off and put them in our pockets. Joe kept his yarmulke on.

"You better take yours off," said Morris.

"Why?"

"Well, for the rest of the world it's only a Friday night."

"For me is Shabbat," said Joe. "And I'll keep it on. Are you scared, Morris?"

"A little bit," said Morris. "But I am more unnerved by your illogical thinking."

"Illogical?"

"Yes. You see: if it's Shabbat, then you must stay at home and do nothing. If it is only Friday, then the yarmulke doesn't really matter. You cannot have both."

"I see," said Joe and took his yarmulke off.

Morris was now even more surprised. We walked the rest of the way quietly.

The bar Morris and I used to go to was close by Morris' University and most of the customers were professors and post-graduates. It was always packed and everyone drank only beer and smoked Dutch tobacco. We found a table and ordered a pitcher.

"So, Morris," Joe said, "why do you dislike me so much and so openly?"

I looked at Joe, at his big, bushy beard, already gray here and there, at his short forehead and his small ears, at his white hands with stubby fingers, so out of proportion with his big and broad body, I looked at him and it felt as if I was seeing him for the first time. He looked back at me and almost unnoticeably smiled. At once I knew that Morris was wrong, very wrong.

"Tell me, Morris: why?"

"Here we go," said Morris. "Let's drink first. Why rush? It might turn out that I don't really dislike you."

"No, Morris," I said. "The man is asking, so tell him now."

Morris looked annoyed with what I said.

"Come on, Morris," I said again. "Tell us why is it that you dislike the man."

"Screw you, Daniel. Why don't you tell him why you dislike him?"

I tried to soften the tone:

"Beside that he is a lousy singer, there is nothing else I hold against the guy," I said.

"Am I a lousy singer?" Joe said.

"Worse than I am, in any case," I said. He smiled at me again.

The Beatles started to play from the speakers.

"Ok, Joe. It's true. I don't like you much. And I'll tell you why," Morris said. "But only if you tell me first this: who is playing now?"

Joe smiled:

"So, this is how it is going to be? 'The Beatles', 'Good Day, Sunshine'."

Morris was surprised again:

"My mistake. This one was too easy. Everyone knows 'The Beatles'. Lucky guess."

Another pitcher arrived:

"Joe, it's not that I dislike you. It's just that you make me angry somehow. You know, the stuff you say and the way you say it."

"Angry?"

"Yeah, angry. You talk like some old rabbi from a shtetl in Poland."

"Perhaps because my father is a rabbi, I am sure you know this. His Father was a Rabbi too. The father of my Zayde, my Bubbie's father, they were both rabbis..."

"But you are not, Joe," Morris said.

"It is true, I cannot deny it. But if I were a rabbi, would it change anything?"

"Change what?" Morris said.

"Would you dislike me more or less?"

Morris took a big gulp from his mug:

"I am telling you: I don't dislike you really. I don't know what it is. You are a nice guy," Morris said.

"I don't think I am a nice guy," Joe said and emptied his mug.

"The Beatles" were still playing. We sat quietly through two songs. Then Joe ordered another pitcher.

"I'll give it to you: I don't know how to make small talk." Joe said. He looked at his beer mug, visibly wandering away. He finally said:

"Ok, my fellow Jews. Let me tell you my life story. It's fairly short.

When I was just a little kid, I knew plenty. I knew then much more than I know now, that's for sure. I knew the Torah by the time I was ten, I knew Mishnah by the time I was fourteen. But I didn't know what to do with it.

One day I met a young couple, my age, in a place just like this. I just turned eighteen. I was already in the rabbinical school. But after I met those two, everything started to look and be different. They were Jews from Israel, a girl and a young man from Kibbutz. We talked about many things. They liked to talk a lot about Spinoza. In the end every time we met, we talked only about him. And when the time came for me to become a Rabbi, I couldn't do it. Instead, I went to Israel with those two. I wrote to my mother and father from the Kibbutz over there. I tried to explain my reasons. But those reasons no one could explain. Whichever way you looked at it, I was only an ungrateful son. I almost killed my mother and my father."

His small eyes wandered away and Morris and I kept quiet. The young women and men stood around us tightly packed, with their beer mugs and rolled up cigarettes. "The Beatles" were not playing anymore.

"I am what they call bipolar now. I take medicine, but it doesn't help much."

We ordered another pitcher.

"What is this, this old stuff?" Morris said.
"'The Platters.' 'To Each His Own,'" Joe said.
"This is very old stuff," Morris said. "How come you know this?"
"I listen to the radio a lot. It's not that old," Joe said.
The Platters kept playing and Joe was telling us the songs' names: "The Great Pretender", "My Prayer", "You'll Never Never Know"…
We got boozed up pretty well that Shabbat. Morris and I walked Joe home. His house was right next to the shul.
"Joe," said Morris, perhaps for the hundredth time that night, "I am sorry, Joe. Didn't mean to be an imbecile."
Joe only smiled while Morris hugged him. Then he put his yarmulke back on and quietly walked to his small, yellow brick house.

I didn't hear from Morris for over a month. Then, as it turned out, he found me in a supermarket, by the bread isle. He saw me from the streetcar, he said, as I was walking into the store.
"I kept calling you the whole week and I called at least ten times this morning. I was on my way to your place now. Ya'akov passed away a week ago. We just finished sitting *shiva*."
"Ya'akov? Who is Ya'akov?" I said.
"Ya'akov Gold. Joe," Morris said and we both cleared our throats.

THE TURNIP AND THE BOAT KNIFE

Daniel woke up suddenly. The December morning was still dark and quiet. A dream woke him up: his mother, who he didn't remember, who died during his birth, called from outside. He looked out through the window and through the door, but he couldn't see her. She called his name with a soft, familiar voice. At once, Daniel understood it was his father's voice. And there, by their old kitchen table, his father and he were standing across each other, just about to cut a turnip. His father said:

"Where is the knife, Daniel?"

Daniel looked behind himself, toward his pillow, turning his head away with a long and slow turn. His father asked again and when Daniel turned back to answer, his father was not there anymore. The whole place had changed. In front of him was a faceless chasm, closing in, growing. It startled Daniel and he woke up.

The turnip Daniel dreamed was from his father's story. The small boat knife with the red handle was his father's present.

Daniel's father was in his mid teens when he got his hands on an old Singer. He quickly taught himself how to measure and cut and sew and he made himself a tailor. He sewed simple summer dresses and bed linen for people who couldn't afford much. In October 1937, just as he turned his eighteenth year, he was taken to Sachsenhausen. There, he was sat behind another Singer to sew shirts and pants for the *lager*. He did it for eight years.

Daniel's father was a good man. He was short and very skinny, always soft and kind in his manner. And he never talked much. The turnip story was the only thing he kept from the lager. A turnip fell off the truck. It fell into snow and no one noticed. He came back for it sometime later, but by then the turnip was already gone.

The boat knife with a red plastic handle was a part of a customer's payment. His father gave it to Daniel for the Bar Mitzvah and Daniel loved it. He kept it under his pillow until it got lost with many other small things that unavoidably disappear over time.

Daniel never married. He blamed his indecisiveness and his lack of talent for speaking for it, but over time he learned how to be content. He learned his father's trade and the two of them grew their shop to eight employees.

Daniel stood up slowly. The parquet was hot under his feet and he suddenly felt a great thirst. He switched on the bathroom light and his father stood there in front of him, small, smiling. A freckled and weak hand opened the tap and water started to rush out. Daniel looked at his father drinking:

"What to cut? Please tell me. I don't know what," Daniel said.

His father looked back from the mirror. He wasn't smiling anymore.

"This is it, Daniel. This is it, my little Daniel. Go back to bed. Everything will be alright."

"This is it?"

"Yes, just go back to bed. It will be very easy."

"I understand: you found the turnip and we will cut it now. We'll cut the turnip. Then let me get my boat knife. It is under my pillow."

THE RED AND WHITE BOBBER

It felt like the cut of a sharp blade, the breath. Then the smell of myrrh, together with fine, almost cold vapors, fell on us, on the old tin boxes with sugar and coffee, on the shaving mirror and on the dark green surface of the small table we painted so long ago. I looked away and through the window. The August day was dragging toward its end, still burning, with little contrast and hope for the consolation of shade, of the smallest movement of air. I remembered fearing this day, and now, when it was here, I stood in it strangely unmoved.

It was a thought that kept me slow and quiet, distant. A thought I am not able to rethink now. It was a thought provoked by something vague yet common, something like looking at the tip of a shoe, or listening to an overly familiar tune. It was as if I were sitting on the riverbank, absently watching the skinny tip of the hazel rod against the quiet water and the red cork bobber with the white stripe I always considered to be a decoration. At the same time this thought carried a definite weight, as if it meant that the memory of our overlapped lives needed time to unravel itself.

I looked at his still chest, at his face already lost forever and there was nothing to be done. I stepped toward the bed and I caught my eyes looking back from the dewed mirror. From its small silver surface, eaten away at the edges, an old man was watching. I made a few more steps across the narrow room, through the myrrh and dew, and I stood by my father until the shadow of our old, barren pear tree threw itself over the window and into the room. Before I pulled the bed sheet over his head, I closed his eyes and I crossed his arms on his ill chest. Then I sat by his feet.

To my father.

CPSIA information can be obtained at www.ICGtesting.com
Printed in the USA
LVOW050754021012

301066LV00001B/10/P

9 781460 203927